DEMONS

Julie Conrad

Published in 2021
by Julie Conrad

© Copyright Julie Conrad

ISBN: 978-1-913898-15-1

Also available as an ebook

Cover and Book interior Design by Russell Holden
www.pixeltweakspublications.com

To my husband Alan Conrad and our family of Pomeranians, Heston, June and Brodie.

PROLOGUE

Patrick did not want to go home but there was nowhere else to go. He despised Annette for what she had said to the police. Did she really think he was covering something up? He might cover for his son, but not for himself. He entered the house; as usual, AP, their lively Labrador, charged towards him and jumped up with excitement.

Life had become a rollercoaster, with great highs and even greater lows.

Dishevelled in a black overcoat, his hair wild and overgrown, he caught his reflection in the mirror.

God, I look old. He retreated to his study with a bottle of vodka, put on the radio – classical music – and shut the door on the world.

'L'enfer, c'est les autres.'

'Hell is other people.'

Jean-Paul Sartre, 1944. *Huis Clos* (*No Exit*).

'If relations with someone else are twisted, vitiated, then that other person can only be hell. Why? Because … when we think about ourselves, when we try to know ourselves … we use the knowledge of us which other people already have. We judge ourselves with the means other people have and have given us for judging ourselves.'

Jean-Paul Sartre, 1976. *Sartre on Theater*.

CHAPTER ONE
1987

Hours later, alone in his study, Patrick rubbed his face and eyes. He must have fallen asleep. Slumped over his desk, he raised his head and tried to focus on the clock. His throat was parched. He reached for a bottle of whisky; the amber liquid burned his throat and set aflame his empty stomach. He moaned like a wounded animal, his senses deadened except for the fire in his gravelly throat. He wanted to scream but his lips remained sealed, pressed tightly together. He forbid the release of any sorrow. He needed to cry; his face distorted but his eyes remained dry. He was the living dead, unable to express emotion. A prisoner in his body, serving time for his sins. His body convulsed and he fell to the floor. He lay paralysed.

His eyes were transfixed. She was here. Victoria stood before him – her light blonde hair, her sparkling blue eyes, and the smile that had captured his heart. His eyes widened and his spirits lifted. Here was the woman he loved – an enchanting, beautiful, talented woman. The one who stole his heart at drama school. She was all he ever wanted. He felt blessed by her presence. He felt alive; his love had returned.

'Vic… Vic…' He tried to reach out to her but remained paralysed on the floor. No matter how he tried, he couldn't move his mouth, unable to formulate the words.

Gradually, her youthful, vibrant appearance began to transform. The eyes that danced began to fade, the open smile replaced with tight, tense lips. His euphoria was dampened by the pain he saw etched on that once beautiful face. A wave of doom washed over him as he was confronted by what had gone before. What he had thrown away.

He closed his eyes, momentarily, jolted and alarmed by the images that flashed before him. Her dead body, a bloody battered mess, the blonde hair blackened by sodden blood. Her face smashed and unrecognisable. He began to scream, scream uncontrollably.

CHAPTER TWO
1986

Annette Preston took a taxi to Manchester Piccadilly train station, to catch the six-fifteen morning train to Euston station. The train was busy. She walked through the carriages and managed to get a window seat; she hoped no one would sit next to her. It had been a while since she had travelled this route. It used to be a regular journey.

'Is this seat taken?'

Annette's pulse quickened. He was about five foot ten, rugged, sexy, collar-length black hair… he looked familiar. His smile unnerved her. She became self-conscious and unsure of herself. He sat down beside her, wrapped in his black over-coat. She noticed a slight smell of alcohol – maybe he had had a heavy night.

The train jolted as it left the station. Annette looked out of the window as the train moved along, stopping at Wilmslow, then Macclesfield station. It picked up speed. Next stop Crewe, on to Rugby, and London Euston.

'Where are you going?' he asked.

'I am going to stay with an old friend. How about you?'

'I live in London. I start a new play at the Hammersmith Armchair Theatre this weekend.'

'What is it?'

'*To Be King*.'

'Oh, my goodness, I thought you looked familiar. You're the actor, Patrick Clarke.'

'Yes, indeed. I am he.'

'As it so happens, my friend lives in Hammersmith, just off Fulham Palace Road.'

'Well, you must tell her or him, you both must come and see the production.'

'I will do.'

They talked throughout the journey, about their careers and interests, and Annette relaxed.

'I've never been married. I have had relationships, but never met Mr Right.'

'I am a widower.'

'Oh, I am sorry.'

'Thank you. It was some time ago. I don't like to talk about it.'

'No problem.'

Tea and coffee were served. Annette had a coffee; Patrick had a juice. She tried to hide her disapproval as he pulled out two miniature bottles of vodka and splashed them into the juice.

'Would you like one?'

'No, too early for me.'

He didn't seem perturbed by her obvious shock. He continued to chat. His voice increased in volume as he downed the drink; other passengers turned around to see who was holding court.

Not long after, he fell asleep.

She needed the loo but would have to wake him as there was not enough space to squeeze past. She decided to wait until she arrived at the station.

* * *

Annette gave him a nudge as the train slowed down and an announcement was made that they had now reached their destination, Euston. Rather groggily, he stood up and reached for his bag. She took advantage of being freed from her seat, got to her feet, pulled on her coat, collected her small case, and bid him farewell.

She joined the queue of people waiting for the train to come to a halt. The Manchester to London Pullman Express rolled into Euston station, and stopped with its customary jolt, which threw all the passengers backwards a pace or two and then forwards. Passengers knew this always happened, but it still seemed to catch them unaware. Doors opened. Everyone quickly left the train and sprinted up the ramp, into the station and off on their way.

Patrick caught up with her on the escalator down to the Tube station.

'Have a lovely weekend with your friend.'

'Thank you. All the best with the play.'

'Don't say that.'

'Oh, I forgot, superstition. Break a leg.'

She took the Piccadilly line to Covent Garden. Once there, she huddled into the large, crowded lift that took them up to ground level, then stepped outside and waited until the crowd dispersed so she could look around for her friend, Liz. It had been an eventful morning so far and she looked forward to a catch-up with one of her dearest friends.

Liz wore a bright yellow trouser suit and stood out like a traffic light. They hugged and burst into conversation.

'Let's go into the General Store Café, it's right in front of us.'

They got a drink and a snack and found a table. It was Friday and already busy even though it was only nine thirty in the morning.

Annette thought how good it was to be back in London. The fast-moving city gave her a sense of freedom and anonymity. That is what she had loved most about London when she had moved there as a student, fifteen years ago. She was able to find out who she was, away from the stifling restraints of family life and small-town mentality.

'So, how is life in Manchester?'

'Okay.' Annette's shoulders slumped.

'Just okay? The last time I visited you in Manchester, you were full of energy and optimism.'

'That's five years ago. I was in a steady relationship and had embarked on what I thought would be an exciting and fulfilling career.'

'I thought you loved your work at the gallery.'

'I do, but there is more to life than work.' She ran her fingers through her hair. 'I want more.' Annette glanced around the café.

'Any chance you might come back to London?'

'No, I couldn't afford to live here. Property prices are crazy.'

'That's a shame, I would love my best friend to live close by.' Liz smiled.

'There is no way I could afford to rent in west London, let alone buy. Enough about me. How are you and Gerry?'

Liz said in a chirpy manner, 'We're good, thank you. He's cooking a special meal for us this evening.'

'Gerry cooks?'

'Yes, you're in for a treat.' Liz gave her a *Time Out* magazine. 'Have a look through that and see if there is anything you would like to do over the weekend.'

Annette realised how much she missed her friend. She was so maternal, always fussed and took care of everybody.

'You decide.' Annette pushed the magazine back to Liz.

'I think we will let Gerry decide. He can chaperone the pair of us over the weekend.'

They took the Tube to Hammersmith, and walked along Fulham Palace Road, towards the house. They passed the independently owned delis and artisan shops, and took a right turn, onto the street where Liz lived, in a mid-terrace property that Liz referred to as her solace.

'Why is the area cordoned off?'

'A young estate agent has gone missing. She had arranged to meet a client at one of the properties.'

'That's terrible. I hope they find her.'

'Women have been told not to go out alone after dark. That's why I thought it best if Gerry accompanies us in the evening. We would probably be okay, the two of us together, but you never know. Until this young woman and her abductor are found, we don't know who we are dealing with. It's a complete mystery.'

'That's fine with me, better to be safe.'

* * *

Annette unpacked a few of her clothes and toiletries. The bedroom was small, tastefully decorated in pale blue with soft blue curtains. It was a bit like a baby's room. She wondered if they planned to start a family. In the late afternoon, she had a nap, then showered and dressed in a pair of relaxed trousers and a sweatshirt.

Gerry fixed them all an aperitif.

'Ladies. Champagne.'

He had set the table in the small dining area.

'Thank you, Gerry. You have made such an effort on my behalf.'

'You're Liz's best friend – she is so pleased you managed to come down to see us. Take a seat.' Gerry disappeared into the kitchen whilst Annette and Liz discussed the state of affairs.

'This AIDS business is scary. It seems to be affecting mainly gay men, in the capital,' Annette said.

'I am glad I'm married. It is dangerous out there these days. You never know where a person has been previously.'

'Apparently the disease is rampant in San Francisco.'

'It is a death warrant, no cure.'

Gerry returned from the kitchen. 'Dinner is served.'

'This meal is sensational. Gerry, where did you learn to cook like this?'

'He has been on a cordon bleu course. I am very proud of him.'

Annette was amazed. She would never consider going on a cookery course. Ever. Yet, here was Gerry, a man, doing just that. The results were superb. Gerry seated himself at the table.

'You seem surprised.'

'I am, truly impressed.'

'Not only is my husband an excellent cook, but he has also arranged this evening's entertainment.'

'Great, where are we going?'

'The Hammersmith Armchair Theatre. Gerry got us complimentary tickets for the premier of *To Be King*. It opens to the public tomorrow. A good line up: May Jefferson, David Reece and Patrick Clarke.'

'Patrick Clarke. Wow, he is rather sexy. You'll never guess who I travelled down with today?'

Gerry butted in. 'If you say so. I think he has had his day.'

Annette continued. 'He has an unkempt look, but he smoulders sexiness. He's so alpha male and his black hair—'

'Dyed, of course.'

Annette was bemused by Gerry's attitude towards Patrick. Might he be jealous?

Liz tapped Gerry's shoulder. 'Don't spoil Annette's image of her idol.'

'He's not my idol.' Annette blushed. She felt like a teenager again, embarrassed.

'What were you saying about your journey down?' Liz asked.

'I've forgotten. It must be great, to work with all those talented actors?'

'They are like a bunch of kids most of the time. They whinge and whine, and actors such as Patrick Clarke are so precious.'

'I am so excited. Thanks, Gerry. I'll nip upstairs and do something with my hair.'

Annette came back in a completely different outfit.

'Wow, you look fabulous. That dress really flatters your figure.'

'Thanks, Liz.'

'I'm going to wear heels too. I'll change into something more glamourous.'

'Don't be too long, the taxi is due soon,' Gerry said.

It was a five-minute journey by taxi, the girls unable to walk the distance in heels. It was busy when they arrived. Gerry fast-tracked them into the auditorium.

'Superb seats, right in front of the stage.'

A bell rang, the lights went down, the curtain raised and act one began. Patrick addressed the audience with a soliloquy.

The actors were so close she could almost reach out and touch them. Her eyes were glued to Patrick. He had such presence, and of course Annette fancied him like mad, more so since she had met him in person. He could have been reiterating jibber jabber and she still would have hung on to his every word. The play was in three acts, Patrick was in all three of them. It had a dark theme, very sinister. As king, Patrick roared out commands to the courtiers, and put to death traitors. The play moved into the third and final act. Annette reflected on how great the day had been, and the weekend was just beginning.

The cast received a standing ovation, and the lights went down.

'We still have time to get a drink or two before the bar closes. The cast will stop off for a drink before they go home, helps them unwind. Right, girls, what will it be?'

'The usual for me, darling.'

'Annette?'

'I would love a Tia Maria and coke, please.'

'Hi, Pam,' Gerry greeted the barmaid. 'White wine and soda, Tia Maria and coke, and a pint of lager for yours truly.'

As they huddled around a little table, Annette kept an eye on the doorway to the dressing rooms.

'Do you and Gerry come here often?'

'Hardly ever. But Gerry's stage manager here for most productions, so we thought we would make the most of his connections, getting the tickets for free.'

Annette noticed some of the actors as they approached the bar.

'Oh, my goodness, it's him, it's Patrick.'

Annette was transfixed. Patrick was surrounded by an entourage. They lit up cigarettes and soon it was hard to see him through the plumes of smoke.

Gerry brought over a tray of drinks.

Annette took a large gulp of her Tia Maria.

Liz rolled her eyes. 'You haven't taken your eyes off him. Don't you think you should play hard to get?'

'Hard to get? He hasn't even noticed me.'

Liz grimaced and sat back in her chair, arms folded.

* * *

The smog of cigarette smoke around Patrick's table had thickened. He was still there holding court.

Gerry returned to the table with another round of drinks and a younger guy, named Jason Hobbs.

'Jason, you know Liz, this is a close friend of ours, Annette Preston.'

'Pleased to meet you.' Jason held out his hand.

'Likewise.'

Annette had one eye on Patrick. As he downed his whisky at a rate of knots, his voice became louder, just as it had on the train. He and his group were chain-smokers, the area around him a hazy blur. Annette was aware she had caught his eye amidst the smoke and revelry at his corner table. His eyes bore into her and she felt the need to look away, unnerved. She could feel her face flush. Self-consciously she tried to engage in conversation with her friend but was unable to take in a word Liz said.

She sensed someone by her side. She instinctively looked up and took a sharp intake of breath. It was him, Patrick, cigarette in hand, looking at her. Annette became paralysed, her body seized up. His unruly black hair had fallen over his piercing blue eyes. She was overwhelmed. Fiercely attracted to his air of decadence and his powerful aura, she found he both unsettled and captivated her. The black suit he wore was crumpled. He suited the crumpled look, it was so him.

Gerry broke the silence.

'Patrick, join us.' Gerry introduced everyone to Patrick and then returned to the bar.

'I feel I have met you before,' he said with a conspiratorial smile.

Liz was won over by Patrick's flattery and he quickly had everyone in hysterics and held everyone's full attention. Annette felt his hand on her knee. He rubbed it gently. She tensed and her heart beat faster and faster, but she said nothing.

The lights at the bar had flashed on and off for last orders a while ago. It was time to leave.

'You're not by any chance Cinderella?'

'What do you mean?'

'You don't need to be home by midnight?'

'No. My name is Annette, as I told you earlier today.'

'I want you all to join me round the corner, a little bar I frequent.'

His entourage had dispersed and just the four of them remained.

Gerry's dislike of the man had evaporated into thin air, so the trio joined Patrick.

'It's so dark in here, I can hardly see where I'm going.'

'Your eyes will adjust. We will have that table.' Patrick manhandled Annette as he assisted her to a seat. Fortunately, she didn't mind.

The bar was a dark, laid-back basement dive. Annette noted it had a dubious clientele. The women who hung around the bar were clearly doing business, and the men in the dark alcoves were doing another kind of business.

'Are we safe in this place?' Annette huddled close to Patrick. She could feel the frisson as their legs and shoulders touched. His lips were only inches from hers.

'Perfectly safe. You don't bother them, and they won't bother you.'

'It's like one of those speakeasy joints, during prohibition.'

'You remember those, do you?'

'I have seen them on television. You are so not funny.'

Liz had drunk too much. She told Gerry to get them a taxi. Gerry and Liz shuffled to the door without a backward glance and disappeared.

Patrick whispered, 'It's nearly three o'clock, come back to my place.'

'I should go back…'

'They've gone without you. You will be locked out, and it's not advisable for you to be out alone in that area after the abduction. Come on, be a devil.'

In the back of the taxi, they had their first kiss. It lasted most of the journey.

CHAPTER THREE

Annette attempted to force her eyes open, but her eyelids would not cooperate. Her head thudded – mouth dry, body sore and fragile, she lay motionless. The hangover of hangovers. *Never again*, she vowed. She craved a cold, sweet drink, and wondered if it would be impolite to call out to Liz to bring her one. Then again, Liz might be fast asleep. They had drunk far too much. She relived the evening in her mind, the theatre, the bar, all those Tia Marias. She smiled to herself as she remembered Patrick joining them, then they had gone to the speakeasy, more drinks. No wonder she felt like death. Her stomach lurched. She remembered she had gone back to Patrick's place. He had lit the open fire and had poured them a brandy or three. The thought of alcohol made her nauseous.

How the hell had she got back to Liz and Gerry's?

Her heart began to thud uncontrollably. She was somewhere she wasn't supposed to be. She rubbed her eyes and tried to focus on her surroundings. She looked around the room and began to remember a little more of the previous evening. The dimly lit and smoky atmosphere, muffled voices, Liz and Gerry leaving, gazing into Patrick's eyes. She had stumbled through the front door, a Victorian semi with high ceilings.

They had gone into a room and although she had been drunk, she recalled the vivid rich colours of the décor and sofa, shades of red and purple, the roaring fire, flames danced and cast shadows on the wall. She must have passed out.

* * *

Annette got out of bed, still fully dressed. She crept along the landing and into the bathroom. She drank straight from the tap and swallowed great gulps of water, which caused her stomach to churn; she was dehydrated, so she forced herself to drink more.

She tiptoed down the steep stairway. The door was ajar; she could hear movement. She peered around the door. Nothing. She entered the room, and looked towards the archway, which led to the kitchen. There was a light on. She felt like an intruder and braced herself as she walked through. Patrick was sitting at the kitchen table. He wore a purple towelling robe and was reading a broadsheet. He looked her up and down from over the top of his spectacles.

'Good morning.'

'Oh, not so loud, please. Good morning,' she said quietly. *Did anything happen between us? Is he hoping I will clear off as soon as?* Although consumed with negative thoughts, she liked what she saw. He was clearly hung-over, but incredibly sexy. She didn't want him to look too closely at her, her skin dry and taut, eyes red, complexion extremely pale. She let her hair fall over half of her face.

'Join me, have some coffee.' He gestured for her to sit down.

'I really should be going. I'm supposed to be at Liz and Gerry's.'

'No such thing as should.' He turned the page of his news-paper.

'I really do need to go.'

'No need to sound so apologetic.' Patrick folded the paper and put it down on the table. 'I'll call you a taxi. I would give you a lift, but we have our first matinee today.'

'The show must go on.' She cringed. He must have heard that a million times.

Five minutes later, the taxi arrived. He took her by the hand and led her to the door. He kissed her on the forehead.

'I will call you this evening.'

'You have Liz's number?'

'I'll find it.'

Throughout the journey from Hampstead to Hammersmith, her thoughts were consumed with Patrick – confused, elated, scared but excited. Why had she rushed away? Why hadn't she stayed for a coffee? Would he call her later?

CHAPTER FOUR

Patrick arrived at the theatre with just fifteen minutes to get to his dressing room and change before curtain-up.

There was a knock at the door.

'Come.'

It was Mike, the floor manager. 'Patrick, there's a call for you.'

He took the call at the payphone attached to the wall in the corridor. As actors rushed by, he checked his watch.

'Darling, I tried to call you at home.'

'Leona, hello, you must have just missed me. I can't talk right now, I'm on stage in a few minutes.'

'Martin's away. Should I drive down today?'

'No, Leona, not this weekend. I have to work, another performance tonight.'

'I don't mind. I just want to see you.'

'No, it's hardly worth it. As I said, I'm back at the theatre this evening, and I need to catch up with some rest. I had a heavy night last night.'

'Martin's away until Tuesday.'

'Sorry, I have to go. Call me tonight, after midnight.'

He jogged down the corridor and onto the stage.

* * *

Leona was disappointed. Martin was away until Tuesday, and she was left with nothing to do. Her life had become so dull. She used to enjoy going to lunch with the girls, unlimited credit card allowance, shopping, beauty treatments, hairdressing appointments. Then there had been the social whirl of dinner parties and charity and gala balls. She and Martin appeared in *Cheshire Life Magazine* almost every month. They had been part of the Cheshire glitterati. It had all come to an abrupt end when she had gone too far. She had brought humiliation on her husband. He was not angry about her affairs with the tennis instructor and personal trainer – it was because she had used Martin's credit card to pay for everyone's fun. She had become careless, shared too many secrets with her fair-weather friends. Because of the increased and ever-growing credit card statements, the accountant had brought the matter to Martin's attention.

* * *

'Martin, I've got us a table.'

'James. Thanks for agreeing to join me for lunch, I have got to talk to someone.'

'I'm always here for you, my friend.'

The waiter approached the table.

'Two glasses of Chablis and I will have a Caesar salad,' Martin said.

'Same for me.' James shrugged and asked, 'What's the problem?'

'It's Leona. I have had enough.'

'Okay.'

'Once upon a time she was the belle of the ball and a great asset to me. Do you remember I used to call her my goddess? Over the years, I have been hurt by her infidelities.'

James nodded.

'I was besotted with her but not anymore. She spends money like water, the affairs. She drinks too much. I get home to find her asleep on the sofa, befuddled with booze, in a track suit. She makes no effort for me. Yet she is dressed to the nines when she returns from her assignations. I'm sick of her. I can't stand to look at her anymore.'

'I must say, Martin, you have put up with a lot over the years. She was always a flirt.'

'She did more than flirt.'

James saw his friend was troubled. 'And you have never strayed?'

'Every man within a two-hundred-mile radius has shagged my wife. She made a fool of me. So yes, I've had my moments, but only since I realised I didn't love her anymore.'

'What will you do?'

'I'm going to rein her in. Reduced the credit limit on the card. I saw a house in Mobberley. I've put an offer in.'

James raised his eyebrows. 'Leona will hate it. It's rural, too quiet.'

'I know, that's why I want to move there. I don't care what she wants anymore. I want her to clear off out of my life.'

The waiter brought their drinks and a bottle of still water.

Martin fidgeted. 'I don't give a damn who she sleeps with.'

'Martin, you know we are all behind you. We know you've had a raw deal. We sympathise.'

'I can't wait to tell her I am going to sell our beautiful home in Alderley Edge and relocate to Mobberley. It will drive her crazy. It's only two miles from where we are now, but it will be like living in the Shetland Islands, as far as Leona's concerned.'

Martin sneered. 'She will be brassed off. She will leave me for someone else – let one of her fancy men foot the bill. I want to start again, with a woman who adores me.'

'Anyone in mind?'

'Not yet. I'd like her to be a younger, more vital woman with all the glamour and beauty Leona once possessed. A woman who will make me feel good about myself. If I could get rid of her, I would have the world at my feet.' Martin looked through the large window at the young women walking by.

'Sounds good, but where would she go?'

Martin's face spoke volumes.

'I don't think any of her men would take her on willingly. But I have got to offload her somehow. There is a world out there, James. I want to be part of it, without Leona. I'm in my forties, business is booming.'

'You would be a catch for any woman. You could have your pick of the gorgeous, younger women looking for a husband.' James wanted to reassure his friend.

'Thanks, I appreciate your support.'

The waiter returned with their salads.

'Some guys, in their fifties and sixties, find it a relief not to have to perform marital duties with their wives – let some other fella do the work for him,' said James.

The waiter topped up their glasses.

'I have had to bide my time. I have had to wait for Leona to stray with a man she wants to keep. Have you heard of the actor Patrick Clarke?'

'Yes, damn good actor.'

'She has been seeing him. He could be the answer to my prayers. He has got what she craves – fame, charisma, sex appeal – and hits the bottle. They are a marriage made in hell.'

Martin and James roared with laughter.

* * *

A few months later, installed in the new house in Mobberley, Leona reflected on her marriage to Martin. They had been married for ten years. It had been good in the early days. Their relationship worked because they never spent a great deal of time together. They always had friends around them or did things separately. He had been happy to indulge his wife with gifts of jewellery, cars, holidays. Martin had changed over the years. Leona could not pinpoint when that change had begun. She knew she had taken her eye off the ball.

Leona persuaded a friend of theirs to meet her at the one public house in the area.

* * *

'Thanks for picking me up. I'm not cut out for a mile trek to a pub of all places.'

'This place certainly isn't you, Leona.'

Belinda looked around the olde worlde public house, with old-fashioned wooden tables and a hearth in the middle of the room. She went to the bar and ordered two white wine spritzers.

'Did you tell James we had arranged to meet?'

'No. He meets with Martin at least once a week, doesn't tell me what they talk about. Not that I am about to take sides. I love you both.'

'I hate it round here. He has locked up my Jag. I'm stranded in no man's land.'

'Bit of an exaggeration. It's not even two miles to Wilmslow and Alderley Edge. Take a taxi.'

'And go where and meet who? The girls have dropped me.'

Leona shifted about on the chair; it didn't stand firmly on the floor. She rocked the chair back and forth to bring to the attention of the barman that the damn chair was wonky.

The barman came over and put a beer mat under one of the legs. Leona gave a desperate sigh. 'I can't believe I am actually sat in this dark and dismal pub. With a beer mat under the chair leg.'

Belinda couldn't resist a giggle. 'If you need any cash?' she said to compensate for her finding Leona's predicament amusing.

'Thanks. He put a limit on the credit card. I might need to borrow a couple of hundred?'

'I'll see what I can do.'

'Thanks, Belinda.'

The barman returned with their drinks and a bowl of nibbles.

'How are you bearing up?' Belinda could see Leona was like a coiled spring.

'I think I might have a way out. I cannot just leave Martin. I have nowhere to go, and he holds the purse strings. But I do have someone in my life.'

'Who?' Belinda leaned forwards over the table.

'Patrick Clarke, the actor.'

'You're a dark horse. How long have you been seeing him?'

'No offence, but I can't divulge too much. If Martin knew for sure, it would give him ammunition. He knows about Patrick, but has no evidence.' Leona took a large gulp of her drink.

'Is it serious?'

'I'm serious. Patrick has a few issues to deal with before we can go public.'

'Such as?'

'I don't think Patrick and I are exclusive.'

'Leona, this doesn't sound a viable solution to your situation.'

'It has to be. I need to get away from Martin. Patrick and I are made for each other. The sexual chemistry is amazing.'

'Oh, Leona, when will you ever learn? Relationships aren't just about sex – otherwise James and I would have parted company years ago. You and Martin have got it all.'

Abruptly Leona said, 'I am forty-three years old. I don't want to go horse riding or walk the dogs, as my neighbours do. I want glitzy wine bars, celebrity-owned restaurants, expensive clothes and jewellery, and lots of money at my disposal.'

'Patrick isn't your salvation. Work things out with Martin, try marriage guidance.'

Belinda was wasting her breath.

'Martin has become an angry, volatile person. I've learned not to say too much to him, unless I've had a drink and then all hell's let loose.'

'You've put him through so much.'

Leona ignored Belinda's remark. 'Patrick has a dark side, which scares me a little. He is very, very sensuous and dangerous and you know how I love a bad boy. I am addicted to him. The sex is incredible and the power he has over me in the bedroom is mind-blowing. Martin is my jailer. He controls what I spend, destroyed my social life. He finds fault in everything I do or say. I stopped wanting Martin years ago. Patrick is my ticket out of here.'

Belinda had heard all this before. 'Someone needs to tell you this and it might as well be me. You are not in your twenties anymore, you are forty-three. You are at a time in your life where you need to ensure you have security. You seem to forget that Martin is your husband. All this talk of sex and bad boys is for the youngsters. Leona, you need to grow up and see what you have with Martin before it's too late.'

'I can do without the lecture. You might be happy to sit in your dressing gown and slippers each evening and endure an unsatisfying sex life and a hot chocolate to keep you warm at night, but that's not for me.'

'It's not unsatisfying. Relationships change as you get older. James keeps me warm with his love and loyalty.'

'It sounds as if you want me to just give up on life. You are welcome to middle age, your "this is as good as it gets" lifestyle attitude, but it's not for me.'

Belinda knocked back her drink. 'Well, I tried to make you see sense. I must get home to my cosy, predictable life, and do you know? I love it. Shall I drop you back at the house?'

'No. I'll walk. I'm in no rush to get back.'

Together they strolled to Belinda's car.

'If you don't change your mind, good luck with Patrick.'

'I don't need luck. Patrick is mine, I know it.'

'Don't be defensive. I don't want to rain on your parade. I care about you.' They hugged.

'Bye, Leona. Take care.'

Belinda drove away, saddened by Leona's situation. She had tried to make her see sense. Belinda decided she would drop Leona as a friend; she couldn't bear to witness Leona's self-destructiveness.

CHAPTER FIVE

'Welcome home, stranger,' Liz said in a tone of disapproval.

Annette gave a tired smile.

'I'm so tired, I think I will try to get another hour's sleep.'

'Didn't get much sleep, did we?'

'Oh, Liz, don't. I'm not a child, but, no, I didn't and not for the reason you are thinking. At least, I don't think it is. I can't remember much after we arrived at his house.'

'How disappointing. You have no memory of the night, at all?'

'No, I think I must have passed out. I awoke fully dressed in the spare room.'

'Are you seeing him again?'

'I hope so. He said he would call me later.' Annette leaned against the doorway.

'Oh.'

'What is it, Liz?'

'Gerry said he isn't the type you should get serious about. What I am trying to say is that he is a law unto himself. He has lots of casual relationships, none seem to last. Gerry says he drinks too much, got a bit of a problem with the booze, and is unreliable. See the guy, but bear in mind he is not the marrying type.'

'Who said I am looking for a husband?' She was furious.

'I'm sorry, it is all coming out wrong. I can tell you have been unhappy with your lot lately. Just don't build up your hopes.'

'You seemed to like him last night.'

'Of course, he is very amusing, but you have to take him for what he is. A fun guy who likes to play around. He is not a keeper. According to Gerry, he is trouble.'

'Gerry appeared to get along with him too.'

'We all had had a lot to drink. Gerry would never be rude to Patrick. The truth is Gerry doesn't much care for the man. There, I have said it.'

'So, because Gerry does not like him, we mustn't like him?'

'Not at all. Patrick has a volatile personality, he can be ruthless.' Liz paused. 'I think I have said enough.' Liz stood up from her chair and walked towards her.

'I think you have. I am not a child. I have had no fun or excitement in my life for a long time. Don't try to spoil it for me.'

'We must not fall out over this, Annette. I don't want to see you get hurt.'

'The only way a person can guarantee never getting hurt in this world would be to retreat into a darkened room and never come out. I prefer to take my chances.'

Conversation was strained between the girls for the rest of the day, avoiding the subject of Patrick Clarke.

* * *

'Annette, a call for you.' Liz gave a nod, to indicate who it was.

'Feeling better?' he asked.

'Yes, much better. How was the matinee?'

'It was fine.' He paused. 'I have been allowed the evening off, the stand-in can shine for tonight's performance. I want to see you.'

'I want to see you too.' Her heart raced.

'I'll drive over and pick you up in an hour.'

'I'll be ready.'

Annette returned to the lounge.

'Patrick said he would pick me up at eight o'clock. I am sorry it's messed up our plans, but…'

'You go. I will watch television alone. Gerry isn't home until eleven thirty.'

Annette knew she had disappointed her friend. They were supposed to be having a catch-up weekend, but she would not be guilt-tripped. She intended to pack as much into the weekend as possible. Going out with Patrick Clarke, on a Saturday night, was a dream come true. Liz had Gerry. She must understand how important this date was to her – she would eventually get over it.

* * *

She considered it a little presumptuous but packed a small overnight bag, to be on the safe side. She heard the car pull up outside the house.

'Bye, Liz.'

No reply. Annette cringed with guilt, then went outside and closed the door behind her. Patrick was in an old, battered BMW 3 Series. He drove them to a vegetarian restaurant, a low key and very friendly place, after which he drove them back to his.

On this second visit to his house and after only two glasses of wine, she was able to view the property clearly. The living room was decorated with luxurious, deep red, purple and green cushions and throws; it had a Turkish feel to it, with the heavy, dark wood furniture. Although it was full of warm colours, there was also a cold, austere vibe. The open fire had depleted to burned embers. He switched on a couple of lamps and found a jazz station on the radio.

He passed Annette a glass of Burgundy wine and joined her on the sofa. He put his arm around her shoulders and brushed her forehead with his lips. It caused her to tingle all over; her breath became slower and deeper. His kisses moved down to her neck and then her collarbone. He slipped his hand inside her blouse. She knew if she held back, the moment would be lost forever.

'Stay the night,' he whispered.

'Yes,' she breathed.

He picked up their glasses and led her upstairs, the house dimly lit, very still. She followed him into the bedroom and looked around her. A large, antique bed sat in the middle of the room flanked by antique cabinets and at the foot of the bed was a large wooden chest, like something off a pirate's ship, from *Treasure Island*. Her shoeless feet sank into the warm, thick pile carpet. Patrick saw her look at an adjoining door.

'It leads to my study.'

She smiled and nodded.

'Come here.' He wrapped his arms around her and gently manoeuvred her onto the bed. His hands explored her body whilst his hot breath warmed the arch of her neck. The moment was interrupted by the telephone. He ignored it, but it persisted.

'I'll take the blasted call in the study.'

'You could ignore it, it's very late.'

'Better not. It could be important. Make yourself comfortable, back in a minute.'

He took the key from the cabinet, unlocked the adjoining door and closed it behind him. On his return he relocked the door, undressed and got into bed with her. The aroma of the candles he had lit filled the cool night air, the flames casting shadows. He took hold of her and pulled her on top of him.

'What was so important?' she whispered.

'What?'

'The call.'

'It was nothing.'

He began kissing her, long passionate French kisses, then rolled her onto her back. He pressed hard against her. Her body responded like it had never responded to anyone before. His lips moved down to her breasts as his hands stroked her inner thighs. His large, hot hands explored every inch of her burning flesh. He pushed himself inside her. He thrust harder and harder. For a moment they caught each other's eyes. There was a look in his eyes she couldn't quite figure out. He gazed into the eyes of someone else, someone he was familiar with. He wasn't making love to her, but someone else, someone he was well rehearsed in satisfying.

* * *

Annette awoke to find Patrick not there. She turned to the clock – eleven o'clock, on a Sunday morning. On reflection, maybe she had overreacted to their first sexual experience together. Perhaps they had both been put off by the telephone call, and that had caused her imagination to run away with itself.

This time she ambled to the bathroom, took a shower, put on a change of clothes, did her makeup in a leisurely fashion.

Did this mean they were a couple? Or were they simply seeing each other? She didn't want to scare him off by appearing clingy. She went downstairs through the living room into the kitchen. No sign of him. She switched the kettle on and had a look through the cupboards. There were the regular staples: tea, coffee, sugar, cereals, tinned stuff. Annette had an uneasy sensation in Patrick's house. She sensed she was unwelcome within these walls. She couldn't relax and had to move around.

She looked out of the kitchen window, onto the back garden and observed the overgrown, unruly foliage. It made her smile; the garden was a representation of Patrick's personality to perfection, his unkempt style of dress and floppy black hair. Amongst all the tall weeds that were blowing in the wind were some beautiful pink and yellow flowers, wild flowers that survived amongst the thistles. A lot could be done to pretty it up; she would love the chance to tidy it and make it special. She decided to give Liz a call. She went through to the hall to the telephone. On top of the phone was a Post-it note. It read,

Annette, I had to dash.
Have a good journey home.
P. x

CHAPTER SIX

Two weeks on, back at work, her weekend in London seemed a long time ago, her whirlwind encounter with Patrick like a dream.

On Wednesday evening, alone at the flat, Annette decided to take a hot bath and have an early night. She picked up a couple of magazines and lay on the bed, wrapped in a cosy old dressing gown. The telephone rang. She rushed to answer it.

It was him.

Annette swallowed hard and her breath became faster.

'Hi.' She tried to sound cool and calm, whilst with a clenched fist her finger nails dug into the palm of her hand.

'Sorry I haven't rung sooner. How are you?'

'Fine, how are you?'

'I'm good. Listen, when are you coming down?'

'Down where?'

'To stay with me?'

Thoughts of an early night were banished. She was energised – no way could she sleep now.

'I could travel down Friday.'

'Why not stay for a long weekend? Stay until Monday or Tuesday.'

The idea of a long weekend with Patrick was very appealing.

'I could ring in sick on Monday morning.'

'Sounds like an excellent idea. I am at the theatre Friday evening, and there is a Saturday matinee. Could you take a taxi over from Euston? Come straight to the house. I will leave the key in the hanging basket by the front door. You can arrive when you choose, no need to rush.'

'Super, I will be at your house, waiting for you.'

'I have to go now, babe. See you Friday night. Sweet dreams.'

'Bye,' she whispered.

* * *

He came out of his study, locked the door behind him and went downstairs.

'Patrick, be a darling and pour me another gin and tonic,' Leona purred.

He poured out two large ones, took the drinks over to the sofa and sat opposite her. Leona was six foot tall, a stunner – long red hair cascaded over her shoulders, her body was slender and toned. She had hazel eyes and a pale complexion with freckles.

Leona wrapped her long slim fingers, which were perfectly manicured, around the glass and stretched back against the sofa, causing her skirt to rise up, revealing her very long legs.

Patrick and Leona had little in common, but there was a chemistry between them that was electric.

Patrick desired her but he didn't like her. He didn't like himself very much.

Leona stood at the foot of the bed, naked, running her fingers through her long hair seductively. He watched her as he downed a triple whisky. Her perfume engulfed and aroused him. Did Leona's husband know she was unfaithful on a grand scale? How many more men had she had? The thought of other men made him strangely jealous. He blotted out those thoughts as a stirring grew within his loins. He closed the bedroom door, lit a solitary candle and placed it on top of the chest at the foot of the bed.

Leona lay back provocatively, her hazel eyes on fire, red hair aflame. It framed her delicate porcelain face. She had a phenomenal body and what she did with it excited him every time he thought of her. She would stop at nothing, which sometimes he was uncomfortable with. Did she like it? Did she do this sort of thing with other men? There was no tenderness between them, it was a physical thing.

Patrick undressed, never taking his eyes off her naked body; her entire being aroused him, taunted him, dared and challenged him. She should never challenge him; ultimately, he was the stronger and he could break her. He could squeeze the last breath out of her if he chose to, and that was the ultimate aphrodisiac.

He stood over her and dropped to his knees, pinning down her arms. He pushed harder and harder, wanting to push the whole of him inside her. He had the power. He was in charge. Leona struggled, her eyes widened. He was on the verge of ecstasy. He saw raw fear in her eyes, but he could not stop, would not stop. She pushed with all her might against him, but was powerless against his demonic strength. The fear in her eyes only served to heighten his excitement, which began to build and build, until he came in a frenzy of mixed emotions, desire, power, fear, and death.

Leona reached for her throat, coughed and spluttered. She grabbed her robe and fled towards the bathroom. She turned and glanced at him, speechless with anger. She slammed the door behind her. He had broken the rules of the game. She had almost been asphyxiated. He could have killed her.

* * *

There was always a war going on within him, tearing him apart. A battle between his conscience and his desires. His desires usually won. He tried to quieten both emotions with alcohol and drugs, but they often only served to exacerbate his self-loathing. He battled daily with his addictions, of which he had many. They blotted out his fear of losing control completely, of self-destruction. He destroyed those around him in order to save himself. It gave him a sense of buying time. Buying time for what? He had no idea.

He pretended he was okay, yet always looked over his shoulder, always afraid. He had no peace.

CHAPTER SEVEN

On Saturday evening, Annette joined Patrick at the theatre. She was allowed to watch him from the wings. To play the part of a king so suited his ego. She marvelled at his energy and stage presence; he was electric, and the audience loved him. He was, indeed, a brilliant actor.

The whole theatrical experience was invigorating. It was make-belief made real.

Back stage was full on – hurried costume changes with the wardrobe assistants, quick repairs of garments torn through being stretched from overuse. The sewing machine could always be heard. The hushed chatter, before sending the actors back on stage.

After three standing ovations, the cast left the stage and went to their dressing rooms. Patrick had a room to himself. He had a bottle of champagne chilling on ice. More champagne was ordered as more people joined them in the small dressing room. Music began to play, and no one left the theatre until two o'clock in the morning.

On Sunday morning, Patrick and Annette took a walk on Hampstead Heath. It was a crisp, fresh, typical autumn day. People were out running, walking dogs, or just taking a stroll.

'Should we get a dog?'

'We?' The word filled her with cosy optimism.

'Yes, why not?'

'Would it live here with you?'

'Well, of course it would.'

She smiled to herself. 'If you got a dog, would it be our dog?'

'Yes.'

Annette linked her arm through Patrick's and snuggled up to him. 'It would be quite a responsibility.'

'Are you implying I am not a responsible man?'

'Are you?'

'I could be.'

'I believe you,' she said, smiling at the prospect of being a permanent feature in Patrick's life.

CHAPTER EIGHT
MANCHESTER

There was a week to go before a major exhibition at Harts Gallery, which Annette and the team had painstakingly prepared and worked on for months. She had been unable to see Patrick. She needed to put in the hours; her own conscience ensured she put back the hours she had taken as sick leave.

The artist, Rupert Stokes, insisted on being hands-on when it came to the curating of the paintings. The team had tried to explain that they should curate, but he was insistent that it be done to his satisfaction. Stokes painted on large canvasses – abstract, vibrant full-on action.

They were powerful images. One needed to sit down to take in fully the energy and power thrown out from the canvass. The bold strokes, of crimson, red and yellow splashes overlaid with dark blue stripes, were striking. They reminded Annette of the colours in Patrick's living room.

The launch was by invitation only. The *Manchester Evening News* and *Cheshire Life Magazine* sent their photographers and journalists along, for publicity.

The guest list included the regular buyers at Harts Gallery, premiership footballers and managers, and chief executives of local businesses and organisations. All the big spenders would receive special treatment. Everyone loved being part of the event.

Margot Trott, the manager of Harts, oversaw the event.

'Serve the pre-show drinks and nibbles.' She clapped her hands at the waiters. 'Come along.' Drinks served, people mingled and viewed the work, whilst waiting for the arrival of Rupert Stokes.

The guests adored being photographed by the newspaper and magazine; they liked to keep their profiles in the public domain.

Annette had invited Patrick, but he was busy with the play. His understudy was ill, and he would have been in breach of contract if he missed a performance for mere social reasons. Plus, the public were buying theatre tickets for the production because they wanted to see Patrick Clarke in the lead role. She felt very proud to be in a relationship with such an eminent actor.

Margot kept an eye on everyone; she personally greeted each guest.

'Margot. He is here.' She broke away from her conversation and moved swiftly to the main entrance to meet Rupert Stokes. Rupert followed her to the elevated stage. Margot took hold of the microphone.

'Ladies and gentlemen, may I have your attention please.'

The crowd made their way to the platform.

'It gives me great pleasure to introduce to you this evening an artist whose art has taken the world by storm. We at Harts Gallery are very fortunate to have the privilege of exhibiting this unique artist's work. The tour opened in the Mayfair Gallery. We secured the second exhibition here at Harts, to ensure our loyal patrons, our regular buyers, have the opportunity to purchase these remarkable paintings, before they go countrywide and on to Europe.

'Ladies and gentlemen, please put your hands together for Mr Rupert Stokes.'

Rupert stepped up to the microphone. 'Thank you for such a warm welcome. It is wonderful to be here this evening. The theme of this current collection is *Power*. Positive, electric visions that will blast your senses.

'This collection is very special to me. I hope it will be to you. Thank you.'

Applause echoed through the gallery.

'Annette, over there, speak with the Cravens, discuss the painting. I think they might be ready to buy.' Margot worked the room whilst she kept staff on their toes.

'More champagne, stop the nibbles,' she instructed the waiters.

'Mr Stokes, join me for a photograph.' Margot and Rupert posed, and got the press and promotion out of the way.

Rupert looked at his watch. 'Margot, I just need a minute.'

Rupert walked across the room towards Annette. 'Annette, could I have a word?'

'Hello, Rupert, I have just secured your first sale of the evening. Rupert, may I introduce you to Mr and Mrs Craven.' Annette stood back.

'Mr Stokes, I think we will invest in more of your work in the future.'

'Thank you so much. I do hope the painting you have bought brings you much pleasure. It has been a delight to meet you both. Unfortunately, I'm on a tight schedule.'

'We understand. It was wonderful to meet you.' They shook hands. Rupert ushered Annette to one side.

'I am delighted with the work you and the team have done with the exhibition. I know I might have got under your feet, at times, but it's important I like the layout of the paintings.'

'We understand. Thank you.'

'I have a long-term plan. I want to open a portfolio of private galleries, over the next few years. If ever you leave Harts, let me know. There will be a vacancy with your name on it.'

'Really?'

'We worked well together. I'm satisfied I could leave my work in your capable hands in the future.'

'I might not be in Manchester for long, but I appreciate the offer.'

'Should your path in life change, get in touch.'

They shook hands and Rupert slipped away.

CHAPTER NINE

Patrick was in his dressing room. He partook of a whisky or two before the performance. Gerry popped his head around the door.

'Patrick, could I have a word?'

'As long as it's not a lecture on the evils of alcohol. The last thing I need is a bloody lecture.'

Gerry knew immediately that Patrick was in one of his obnoxious moods. Normally, he would have kept away, but he had promised Liz he would speak to him. Patrick was bad news. When he was drunk, he was unreliable and could be thoroughly nasty, and often was. He was, however, a brilliant actor and the public loved him. So, his bad behaviour was tolerated.

'Patrick, I know it's none of my business, but I promised Liz I would speak to you.'

'Liz,' he repeated in an aggravated tone.

'Liz, my wife, good friend of Annette's. She was responsible for the two of you meeting.' Gerry was trying to be diplomatic.

'Oh, that Liz,' he bellowed. 'Yes, I remember. What is it you want to say?'

'Since Annette has been involved with you, she doesn't seem to want to spend any time talking with Liz. You know, to discuss things, share things, women's talk. Liz is worried Annette will get hurt.'

'Hurt, hurt?' He belted out the words.

'Well, you can understand her concerns.'

'Ask your wife to stop playing mother goose. Annette is a grown woman and doesn't have to report back to your busybody wife, nor does she need her permission to be in a relationship with me.'

'Now, hold on, you're out of order.' Gerry rose to his feet.

'No, you're out of order. Keep your nose out of my business.'

'You are a shit. I don't know what she bloody well sees in you.'

'I think you know exactly what she sees in me.' He fixed Gerry with a hypnotic stare. 'Is this jealousy your wife's or yours? I told you I have no interest in you now nor will I have again. It is over. Get used to it.'

'You bastard.'

'Get out of my dressing room. Now.'

Lost for words, Gerry stormed out of the room.

* * *

Patrick poured himself another large whisky whilst he mumbled a few obscenities. There was a tap at the door.

'What now?'

'It's only me, Justin. Who's rattled your cage?'

'Come in, come in.'

Justin was a young actor and part of the cast.

'Oh, Justin, your timing is perfect, I need to be calm.' Patrick leaned back in his chair and closed his eyes.

Justin obliged and began to massage Patrick's scalp. 'There, there, let's soothe away all that tension.'

'My dear Justin, what would I do without you?'

Another rap at the door. 'Five minutes to curtain-up.'

Patrick began to psych himself up for the performance. He opened the door to leave but turned to take a last look at himself in the mirror.

'Do I look regal enough to be king?'

'Indeed, you do, Your Majesty.' Justin gave a mock bow.

Gerry passed the doorway and caught a glimpse of Patrick taking Justin's hand in his as he raised it to his lips, whilst they gazed into each other's eyes. The moment of intimacy was broken. Patrick dropped Justin's hand abruptly and walked through the doorway, knocking Gerry slightly, on purpose, as he passed.

* * *

Annette and Patrick's relationship was in its third month. She travelled to and from Patrick's house on a regular basis; this had become routine. She would arrive, take the key from the hanging basket and let herself in. It all seemed so natural to do so. Because of Patrick's work commitments, she had spent many an hour alone in the old Victorian house. Alone in the house, she was always on edge; she was unable to find a place within the house where she could relax. There was a presence that unnerved her; it was everywhere. A presence that would not allow her to settle. She would move from the living room to the kitchen. A coldness would envelope her, so she would move again and again.

At two o'clock, Annette arrived at the house, pushed open the door and put her holdall on the chair in the hall. She needed a coffee, so she went to the kitchen and put the kettle on. As she took the coffee and sugar from the cupboard, she heard a noise, then footsteps. She stopped what she was doing and held her breath and listened. She crept through the archway, into the living room. There was noise coming from upstairs. There was someone upstairs. Perhaps Patrick was home early. She called out a hello, and made her way upstairs and listened carefully. The footsteps stopped, but there was a muffled sound, then nothing. She had to check it out and so tiptoed along the landing. She opened the bedroom door and peered in. Nothing. The door to the study was locked as usual. She walked towards the bedroom at the bottom of the landing. It was empty. Another door was also locked.

'Who the hell are you?'

She nearly jumped out of her skin. She turned around to see a semi-naked young man leaning out of the bathroom.

'Who am I? Who are you?' she asked.

'I bloody well live here,' he answered. 'Anyway, what is it to you?'

As the initial shock wore off, she realised she was in no danger. It was obvious to her by the resemblance.

'Are you Patrick's son?'

'Yes. Who are you?'

'I'm Annette Preston, a friend of your father's.'

'A friend, you say? I can imagine what sort of friend you are.'

'I beg your pardon?'

'Look, Annette, or whoever you are, I am home on leave from university, not that it has anything to do with you. I would appreciate it if you would stay out of my way. This is my parents' home, my home, it is not an open house for any old floozy my father decides to drag in. Got it?' He went back into the bathroom and slammed the door behind him.

Speechless, she rushed downstairs and grabbed her coat. She was about to go out when she thought, *where will I go?* Patrick knew she was arriving today. She would wait in the room at the front of the house; she would be able to look through the window and wait for Patrick to come home. She would keep out of the way of his son. Why had he not told her he had a son? He must have known he would turn up sooner or later. He clearly had not told his son about her. Floozy indeed. What was all that about?

* * *

She was cold, so she sneaked out to the kitchen and made a hot drink and took a couple of biscuits. She returned to the room at the front of the house and closed the door behind her. She reflected on her brief encounter with Patrick's son, who had been so rude to her. He looked very much like his father – same dark hair, but less rugged and, of course, younger. He had finer features, and was taller than his father and a good twenty pounds lighter.

An hour passed. It seemed longer, still no sign of His Majesty. She heard footsteps. He clearly wanted her to know he was around and that she was to keep out of his way. She was not about to disappoint him.

She heard him go to the kitchen so she put on the radio – then he would know where she was, and he could keep out of her way. She must have walked to and from the window a hundred times before taking a seat by the fireplace. Patrick never used this room. It was neatly furnished, quite twee, different from the rest of the house. It was the only room where the sun shone through and lit up the space. The walls were painted in magnolia; there were no paintings or pictures, no photographs. In fact, there were no photographs or memorabilia throughout the house. This room felt as if it didn't belong to the rest of the house. There was nothing of Patrick about it. It was most unwelcoming, and although it got the sun, she sensed it was a room full of sadness.

Someone shuffled outside the door. It began to open slowly. As a face appeared, they both jumped. It was the face she had seen on the landing earlier.

'I'm waiting for Patrick. Is it okay to wait in here?' She tried to sound friendly.

The young man stared at her and replied, 'Yes. Tell me, how did you get in?'

'I used the key, from the hanging basket. Your father knew I would arrive today.'

'Right. Who are you?'

Annette wondered what sort of game he was playing. She had already introduced herself. Still, as he now behaved in a civil manner, she would humour him.

'Annette Preston, a friend of your father's.'

'How long have you been his, er, friend?'

'Three months, one week.'

He smiled. 'Oh, it's like that, is it? In that case my father is a lucky man. Tell me, what on earth is it you women see in him?'

What does he mean? 'You women'? How many had there been?

She began to warm to him. After all, he had Patrick's good looks and mannerisms. He even sounded like him, but less of a growl and a few decibels quieter. She smiled back at him.

'I am Matthew, son of Patrick, more's the pity.'

'Why do you say that?'

He must have picked up on her concern. 'Take no notice, only a joke. I am at the Royal Academy of Dramatic Art, RADA – you can imagine, I have a lot to live up to.'

Annette nodded in understanding.

'Dad will be home soon. I'm off now. Feel free to move around the house. You don't need to hide away in this sad room.'

'What do you mean? You described the room as sad. That is how I sense it to be.'

Matthew's eyes darkened. He looked grief-stricken.

'Have I said something wrong? I didn't mean…'

'No, it's okay, you're right, I said it myself, it is a sad room…' There was an uncomfortable silence.

'Anyway.' He collected himself. 'I have to go, probably see you later.'

He was gone. She watched him walk down the garden path. Now she had the house to herself, she would have another coffee.

* * *

She settled down at the kitchen table, with another coffee, and picked up the *Times* newspaper. It was the same old news: war, death, and sadness. *Sadness*, she thought. The toaster popped up. She buttered the toast whilst she daydreamed about the wonderful future she would have here with Patrick, as they shared their lives together. An idyllic future with dogs and cats and long walks on the heath and cosy evenings by the fire. Annette jumped as she saw Matthew leaning against the wall, staring at her, arms folded, with a hostile expression.

'You're back soon,' she said, smiling but confused by his manner.

'What are you talking about? I've not been anywhere. You're still here, I see.' He continued to stare at her. Perhaps she had upset him, by going on about the room being sad.

'I think Patrick will be home soon. As I said, he is expecting me.'

'So, you are the old man's latest? I don't know how he keeps it up – a lot of stamina, has he? The old stallion.'

'I beg your pardon?' She was speechless, again.

'Shall I repeat what I said?'

'Most certainly not. I will get out of your way. I shall go back to the front room.'

'Who said you could use that room? That room is private. You keep out of that bloody room.'

Annette burst into tears; she was confused and frightened by his behaviour. The front door slammed shut. She heard male voices. Patrick appeared, ruffled and unshaven.

'What is going on here?'

'Your son, Matthew, your son… he…'

'Matthew? Matthew, get yourself here now.'

Matthew appeared by his father's side. Annette was taken aback. There was two of them. They were twins.

CHAPTER TEN

Over the Christmas break, the boys were home. Sometimes they stayed out all night and they were out most of the weekend, but, nonetheless, they were around. This changed the dynamics of homelife. Annette did feel she had an ally in Matthew, though he remained guarded about the family history. But now and again he would let something slip. He still made the odd jibe at his father. He tried to be as different from his father as he possibly could.

His twin brother, Geoff, was a different story. He was very much like his father on the surface. Frequently drunk, or high on something, always ready to speak his mind. He made it his business to be as rude and obnoxious as possible. At times, it was as if he hated his father; maybe he did for some reason. What shocked her was how Patrick tolerated the verbal abuse from his son.

* * *

She was still in the process of unpacking her stuff and the recent hostilities had made her cautious about staying. However, she had taken leave from work and didn't relish the idea of returning home to spend Christmas on her own. So, she unpacked.

The play at the Hammersmith Armchair Theatre had finished a week ago. Patrick had a new script to read for the new year, for a play in the West End. He was moody; he drank a lot. The telephone was ringing all the time, which he chose to ignore, or he would pick up the receiver and put it straight down. It troubled her.

'Why am I being kept in the dark? Who is ringing the house?'

'Nothing for you to worry about.'

Annette put up a Christmas tree and decorated it with twinkling lights, but no other effort had been made to make the home more festive. A number of Christmas cards arrived, mainly for the boys. No plans had been made to go out to celebrate or to meet up with anyone – not that she knew anyone locally. It would probably be a trip to the pub and evenings by the fire, whilst Patrick carried on his merriment with alcohol. This suited Annette; she preferred not to share Patrick at this special time of the year.

'I need to go out, won't be long. On no account answer the telephone,' Patrick told her.

She nodded and went upstairs to lie on the bed and read a book. She rolled over and the book fell to the floor. She bent over the bed to pick it up, and noticed something small and frilly. She reached under the bed and pulled out a pair of briefs – to be more precise, a red, tarty G-string.

Her heart sank. Had another woman been in this bed? The same bed she lay on. As the blasted telephone began to ring, she wondered if the owner of the knickers was the caller.

She went back downstairs, her stomach in knots. She joined Matthew in the kitchen.

'Would you like a coffee?'

'No, thank you.' Obsessed about the knickers, she fretted.

'Matthew, I need to ask you something.'

'If it's about Dad and the phone calls, don't bother.'

'What makes you say that? How did you know what I was going to ask?'

He remained silent.

'Is he seeing someone? Is that her on the phone?'

'Him, her. What does it matter? He will never change. What the hell do you see in him? Why don't you find someone else? He's bad news.'

'What do you mean, him or her? Is he seeing someone else?'

'Ask him.' Matthew picked up his cup and went into the living room. Annette followed him, almost hysterical.

'Look, I am sick of doing his dirty work. You need to confront him, not me.' He took himself off upstairs.

The phone began to ring. She jumped. Geoff appeared, with his arrogant attitude; he completely ignored her. He picked up the receiver. She took an intake of breath, then gave a sigh. The call was for him.

The knickers had put a dampener on the afternoon. She had no idea what went on when she was back home. She so wanted to trust him, but he was a free agent. It was not as if they were engaged; the relationship was in its infancy.

Patrick arrived home. As soon as he walked through the door, she pounced.

'I need to speak to you.'

This was going to be unpleasant, but she needed to know. He threw off his coat and sat down by the fire.

'I'm listening.'

'Are you having an affair?'

He began to roar with laughter, whilst tears ran down her face.

'Are you?'

'No need to shout. No.'

She had not expected such a simplistic answer. 'I found a pair of women's knickers under the bed.'

'Oh, no. You've discovered my secret.' He burst out laughing. He leaned back on the sofa and looked at Annette, who was in a state of high emotion.

'I don't find it amusing in the slightest. Who do they belong to?'

'For goodness' sake, it's a joke, you sound like a jealous child.'

Annette stamped her feet. 'Answer me. Is she the one who rings the house relentlessly?'

'I have no idea who they belong to. Could we, please, move on from this?'

'I need to know who they belong to.'

'Did you answer the phone when I told you to leave well alone? Did you?'

'No.'

He stared at her for some time, furious, then he changed his tone of voice.

'Come and sit by me.' He looked into her eyes and gently said, 'I have no idea whose they are or where they came from. Perhaps one of the boys had a girl over.'

'But they were under your bed.'

'Maybe they wanted to use a double bed. Or maybe, just maybe, it's one of Geoff's sick jokes.'

'He might have planted them there deliberately?'

'He could have.'

'What if he didn't? They might belong to some woman you knew before me.'

'How can they? I have never seen them before.' He paused. 'All I can say, hand on heart, is that I don't know how they got there.' He smiled to himself.

'What's so amusing?'

'Nothing you would understand, my darling.'

'And the phone calls? The calls I am not allowed to answer?'

He took her hand in his; he frowned. 'I didn't want to tell you this, but as you keep asking, I guess I must.'

Annette could tell this was something serious. 'Go on.'

'I haven't mentioned it before because I didn't want to upset you. After all, you are a close friend of Liz and Gerry's.'

'Liz and Gerry? What have they to do with this? I haven't been in touch with them for months.'

'I bet I can guess why. It is because of me. Am I right?' He bowed his head.

'How did you know?'

'Gerry pesters me about you.'

'Pesters you?'

'He has been giving me a hard time about our relationship. They think I should stop seeing you.'

'How dare they. How long has this been going on?'

'It began shortly after we got together. I decided not to tell you. I thought you might not believe me.'

Annette calmed down. 'Why would I not believe you?'

'Because they are your friends, who think they have your best interests at heart. I told Gerry you are a grown woman, able to make up your own mind. It appears they don't agree.'

'That is the reason I stopped speaking to Liz. She repeatedly said she didn't want me to get hurt. I think she is jealous.'

'Gerry gave me earache at the theatre. Now I have finished the play, he can't get to me, and they have resorted to nuisance phone calls.'

Annette got to her feet. 'I will go and see them, have it out with them, put an end to this ridiculous behaviour.'

'No, that is exactly what they want you to do. Don't let them see that they have got to us.'

'How many times has Gerry tried to persuade you to stop seeing me?'

'Too many times to recollect.'

'So, they are responsible for these relentless calls?'

He nodded.

'I find it hard to believe.'

'Well, it's the truth. I want you to promise that you will not attempt to visit or call them, and on no account pick up the phone. We must stick together on this.'

'It's crazy.'

Patrick stood up and walked towards Annette. He gave Annette a pleading look. 'Promise me. If you love me you will promise, you will do as I ask, always.'

Annette heard the word 'love', and all reason went out of the window. 'I do love you. I promise, I promise.' She hugged him tightly.

The phone began to ring.

'Stay here, I will deal with this.'

* * *

Patrick closed the door behind him.

'Hello.'

'You bastard.'

'Leona, what do you want now?'

'I want you.'

Patrick hesitated. She always unleashed an erotic charge, a need within him, so powerful it scared him.

She aroused a dark side, a side of him he never knew existed until he met her. It disgusted him. He was disgusted with himself. Next time he might kill her. He didn't want to kill her.

'Patrick, please, say you will see me again. I need you. I feel I will die if I don't have you.'

'What about last time?'

'I forgive you, darling.'

God, no, he thought, as he began to give in to her.

'I beg you, Patrick. Please, please, I will do anything for you. Anything you want.'

'Stop.'

'No, I will never stop. I know you feel it too. I would die for you, Patrick.'

'You would die for me?'

'For you, yes.' She started to laugh.

'Don't laugh. It's nothing to laugh about.'

Against his better judgement, he said, 'Call me at the weekend.' He put down the receiver.

Annette looked up as he returned to the living room.

'It doesn't look as if they are about to give up.' He shrugged.

Manchester was cold and wet. It was January, the longest month.

Liz had left a couple of messages on the answer machine, but Annette deleted them. She had no intention of listening to a load of rubbish about the man she loved. Why on earth would they want to destroy what she and Patrick had? There was more to this than Liz and Gerry's concern for her well-being. There was something not right about it.

Annette felt good about the relationship and wanted to focus on the future; nobody was going to get in the way.

At Harts Gallery, two more exhibitions were in the diary to be curated. Which would require numerous meetings and visits to the artists. Paintings would be viewed; Annette and the artist in question would have to agree on the selection. The theme was freedom. The team would have to work flat out. That suited her; it would fill the days and the evenings. Since she and Patrick had become a couple, she found she enjoyed the work – she was fired up again.

Patrick had reignited her life; she had a passion for him and for art. This was what she had needed, a relationship with someone special. A future with unknown possibilities.

CHAPTER ELEVEN

Patrick, bleary eyed, stumbled upstairs with a tray of tea and toast.

'Get the door for me, Geoff, I've got my hands full.'

Geoff pushed open the door. He glanced into the room and saw Justin, propped up by two large pillows, in the old antique bed. He gave his father a look of loathing. He went downstairs to join his brother.

'I hate him sometimes.'

Matthew looked up from his magazine. He said nothing.

'Guess who he has in his bed this morning? Not happy to screw that slut Leona, and Little Bo-Peep.'

'Little Bo-Peep?'

'Annette, the dozy mare. She believes everything he tells her.'

'He is a good actor. I think Annette is the best of the trio,' Matthew said.

'I despise her gullibility – she is so trusting, she makes me sick. Anyway, guess who's up there?'

'I would rather not know.' He returned to the magazine.

'Justin. Can you believe it? I think I am going to throw up.'

Matthew looked out of the window, as if some sort of answer might be found there.

'I will be glad when I finish university. Once I have a job, I won't need to come back here anymore,' Geoff said.

Matthew frowned. 'If Dad chooses to be with Justin that is his business, and it is his house.'

Geoff responded aggressively. 'Can you hear yourself? Justin, for goodness' sake. There is all this AIDS stuff going around. He goes from Justin, then Leona and then Annette. He is irresponsible.'

'I hear what you are saying. If it bugs you so much, you could always stay with Grandpa?'

'Grandpa hates Dad more than I do. In fact, Grandpa hates Dad with such venom, I sometimes feel the need to defend the old git. I don't, of course. Good grief, if Grandpa knew the half of it.' He pointed upstairs.

Matthew looked at Geoff. 'He is our father, he is all we have, and he is part of us, whether we like it or not.'

'I am going to make him pay for his indiscretions, pay through the nose. I have had a hundred quid out of him this week.' Geoff smirked. 'I might ask him to pass that Leona tart on to me. She might have turned forty, but she is fit.'

'God, you sound just like him.' Matthew cringed.

'Er, no. I draw the line at Justin.'

They both laughed, but their conversation was interrupted by the phone ringing. Geoff went to answer it.

'Hi, it's Annette. Is your father around?'

'Yes, but he is indisposed. He is with a fellow actor, rehearsing in the bedroom. Better not disturb them. I will tell him you called.'

Geoff put down the receiver and turned to his brother.

'Well, dear brother. I think that warrants at least twenty pounds from Father. Another lie, on his behalf. It's a lucrative business.'

* * *

Annette picked up her mail. One of the letters had a London postmark. She opened the letter, and immediately noticed its briefness. It read:

> Annette Preston, keep away from Patrick Clarke, or you will regret it. I know where you live. You have been warned, I will be watching you.

Who would send this? Then she thought of what Patrick had told her. Liz and Gerry might have given Patrick a hard time, but this was going too far. Educated people behaving in this manner. Liz and Gerry, would they do this? Or would Matthew and Geoff be capable of stooping so low? The sooner she spoke to Patrick, the better. Why couldn't people leave them alone?

CHAPTER TWELVE

Annette spoke to Patrick. She insisted she return to London the following weekend. She told him about the letter. Patrick tried to lay the blame on Gerry and Liz, but she was having none of it. It had to be someone close to Patrick.

'Liz wouldn't do this.'

'I think it is Gerry. He gave me a hard time, I told you. He even threatened me.'

'Gerry threatened you? Why on earth didn't you tell me? I find it hard to believe he would go so far on my behalf. I should speak to Liz.'

'Don't involve her. Let me sort this out. You just get yourself down here on Friday evening, don't worry.'

But Annette did worry.

Patrick was at the Old Vic. He summoned Justin to his dressing room. Justin arrived flushed; he was nearly due on stage for act three.

'Patrick, what is so important it can't wait?'

'I have to confide in someone. I have a friend, who lives in Manchester, who has received hate mail.'

Justin looked confused. 'Hate mail?'

'The letter warned her to keep away from me.'

'But why?'

'"Why?" indeed. The sender must be someone who doesn't like me.'

'How can you be sure? It could be someone who cares for you deeply, who wants to look out for you. Scared they might lose you.'

'The woman is no threat. We are merely friends. I have a feeling I know who sent the letter.'

Justin was flustered; his face reddened.

'Surely you don't suspect me?'

'No,' Patrick lied.

'I am about to go on stage. We can discuss it later.' Justin ran down the corridor.

* * *

After the performance, Patrick and Justin sat in the dressing room.

'Ask yourself, who is antagonistic towards me?'

'Quite a lot of people,' Justin answered.

Ignoring his remark, he carried on. 'Think carefully. Who has really got up my nose over the past few months?' Patrick leaned back and slightly slid down in the chair.

'The stage manager, Gerry Scott.'

'Precisely. You have answered my question.'

'I have? Are you sure?' Justin said.

'Quite sure. If anything should happen to me, you are privy to whom is the protagonist.'

'What do you mean "anything should happen"? You don't think he is capable of violence?'

Patrick remained silent.

'You don't think he would take out his hatred of you on me? I was pretty rude towards him, but only because he disapproves of our closeness.'

'Who knows what he is capable of,' Patrick replied, observing the fear in Justin's eyes. A voice spoke from the doorway.

'Justin, Jason wants to see you. Just passing on the message,' Gerry said.

'Aah…' Justin was as white as a ghost. He fled.

Gerry stared at Patrick, then walked away.

* * *

Patrick went backstage and caught Gerry's eye. They didn't speak; they never did these days, unless it was unavoidable. What was Gerry doing at the Old Vic? Why did he need to hang around here? Patrick gave him a knowing smile. Gerry looked uncomfortable. He made for the exit.

Patrick thought the letter business was something and nothing. Probably Justin's jealously getting the better of him. Or Gerry unable to let go.

He decided he would give Annette a surprise at the weekend to take her mind off the letter. It would be an extra-special surprise.

* * *

Friday morning was bright and sunny. Annette opened the window and could instantly feel a crispness in the air. It was so good to be alive. She had taken a day's leave, so she could get down to London. This weekend would start on a Friday. She showered and dressed in a casual outfit. She would take the ten o'clock train, avoid the rush hour. She ran downstairs full of anticipation for the weekend ahead. Three letters lay on the door mat: two brown envelopes, bills no doubt, and a small white envelope, the same as the poison pen letter. Her heart started to thud. She picked up the white envelope and forcefully tore it open, splitting the envelope in two. A small piece of paper floated to the floor. Handwritten, much the same as before.

Annette Preston, keep away from Patrick.

I hate you.

He will always be mine.

This is your last warning.

She began to shake, eyes brimmed with tears, her joy snatched away. Who was behind these letters? How did they know where she lived? Had she been followed? The postmark was London. Patrick had to take this seriously. They had to find out who was sending them or else she would have to inform the police.

CHAPTER THIRTEEN

Patrick received a standing ovation. The rest of the cast joined him to rapturous applause. He loved the adulation but found it hard to keep up the pace these days.

Elated, he returned to the dressing room where the champagne began to flow. More of the cast and the backstage team joined him. Patrick was where he most loved to be, intoxicated and the centre of attention. The party spilled into the hallway and on into the other dressing rooms. When it was time to lock up the theatre, they all moved on to the out-of-hours bar. It was two in the morning before they gradually began to dwindle away. Patrick took a taxi and dropped Justin off en route. They were both very drunk and carefree.

'I love you, Justin.'

'I love you,' Justin slurred.

Patrick needed reassurance. He clutched Justin's hands. 'Do you really love me?'

'Yes, there is nothing I wouldn't do for you.'

'Nothing?' Patrick tried to focus.

'Nothing, you only have to ask.'

Reassured, he bellowed to the taxi driver, 'Home. On to Hampstead.'

He returned home to find Annette asleep on the sofa. Well, she was asleep until he slammed the door and woke her. She rubbed her eyes and looked at the clock. It was gone three in the morning. He walked heavily into the room, knocked a chair over and stumbled. He observed Annette's expression of concern. He put his finger to his lips. *Shh…* He swayed slightly.

'Shall we have a drink?' He ambled to the drinks cabinet. She followed him.

'You're drunk.'

'I am?' He continued to sway, as he poured a brandy. 'What will you have, my dear?'

'I don't want anything. I have waited for you for hours. Where have you been all this time?'

'I-I, my dear, have been at the theatre.' He stumbled backwards a few steps, and then started to laugh uncontrollably.

'You are drunk.'

'I am drunk.' He laughed louder.

She took him by the arm and led him to the sofa. She picked up her bag and pulled out a letter.

'I received another letter this morning. I think the sender is an ex-girlfriend of yours.'

Patrick roared with laughter. He rolled onto his side and held on to his stomach. Tears streamed down his face.

'It's not funny. Read it.'

He took hold of the letter, held it close to his face and then held it out before him. He was unable to focus. She snatched the letter out of his hand.

'I am not going to get any sense out of you tonight, or should I say this morning.'

Patrick was splitting his sides. She went to make him a black coffee.

He awoke on the sofa. His head thudded and his throat was as dry as the desert. He staggered to the kitchen and got himself a glass of water, and then another. The water sloshed around his stomach. He felt he was going to be sick. He remembered Annette was there this weekend – the least he could do was tidy himself up and give her some of his time. With great effort, he showered and dressed, and then went downstairs to make tea and toast. He invited her to join him for breakfast.

* * *

They sat at the kitchen table.

'Okay, shall we talk? I was steamers last night, but I remember the letter. Let me see it.'

'As I said last night, I think it is someone you know, who is jealous.'

'I disagree. I cannot think of anyone who would do this.'

'Read it again. It clearly indicates that it's someone who knows you.'

'Or that is what they want you to think. It could be someone who knows you.'

'Oh, come on, don't start the Gerry and Liz thing again.'

'Before you start telling me what a decent chap Gerry is and how happily married they are, let me tell you different.'

'Go on then.' She looked him in the eye, her arms folded.

'For a start, he turned up at the Old Vic, presented himself at the door of my dressing room. He was creeping around, frightened the life out of Justin. There was no reason for him to be there.'

Annette found this strange. Gerry didn't work there.

'I don't want to taint your simplistic opinion of dear old Gerry and his wife, but he is not Mr Perfect. Do you really think he is happy married to that bore, old Mother Goose?'

'How dare you.'

'I do dare. If he lived in marital bliss, he would never have cheated on her.'

'I don't believe you.'

'He's cheated on her more than once.'

'Stop. This is ludicrous.'

Patrick pulled her towards him. 'Why? Because you choose not to face the truth? Maybe that is why they have tried to destroy what we have. So you wouldn't find out about their sham of a marriage.'

'I can't take much more of this. They would be taking things to an extreme, to resort to hate mail, in the hope we would split up so I would never know about Gerry's extramarital affairs. Please.'

She was tired of the nonsense.

'There is an awful lot more to this than you are willing to accept. You told me yourself that Liz tried to put you off me, because of things Gerry had told her. He has fed her stories of my poor character.'

'Yes, but…'

'We can see where Liz's poor opinion of me comes from, gossip from her husband.'

He embraced her. With his arms around her waist, he spoke quietly. 'Even after what she told you, you still took a chance on me. Liz will not leave it at that. She will continue to bully you until you stop seeing me. Yes?'

'Yes, sort of.'

'The reason she keeps on at you is because Gerry keeps on at her.'

'Why?'

'He doesn't want his wife to know about his latest conquest.'

She began to doubt herself again. 'Do you think Liz knows Gerry has been unfaithful? She has never given me the slightest indication that anything is wrong.'

'She might. She will know something is not right between them.'

'Suppose this is true and Gerry has sent the letters, do you think Liz would know about it?'

He shrugged. 'You are beginning to see the light.' He pinched the bridge of his nose as if he had a headache forming. 'Gerry wrote the letters, implying it was someone who knew me to throw us off track. I know what he is really like, what he is capable of. I have worked with him on a day-to-day basis. You only know him through Liz.'

'What a manipulator.'

'Do you now understand why I don't want you to contact Liz? She might be part of it. Leave it to me. In the meantime, ignore the letters. They are only threats, after all. Perhaps he is jealous because I have you.'

Annette laughed. 'I doubt that.'

'Don't be so modest, you are beautiful. You outshine his wife. And I have a surprise for you.'

'You have?'

'I need to take a short car journey. I will drop you on the heath.'

She waited whilst Patrick drove down the road. She reflected on what they had discussed earlier. As crazy as Patrick's theory was, she was going to trust he was right. She was going to trust the man she loved.

Ten minutes later the battered old BMW approached, chugging up the hill. He parked up and got out of the car. Patrick beckoned her to the rear door of the car. She looked in to see, snuggled up, asleep, wrapped in a blanket, the sweetest little puppy she had ever seen.

'Patrick, he is beautiful.'

'He is, and he is ours. We need to think of a name for the little chap.'

'Snuggles,' Annette suggested. Her anger at Patrick for his night on the tiles and the letter was forgotten.

'I was thinking, AP – A for Annette, P for Patrick.'

'Yes, that's perfect. Is he a Labrador?'

'Yes, I went to look at the litter a few weeks ago. He is one of eight puppies. I reserved him straight away. They are all going to their new homes, three went yesterday. I chose him for his cheeky playfulness.'

'I am so happy he is part of our little family. How will you manage when I am in Manchester?'

'I asked if the boys would help out should I need to be out of the house more than a couple of hours.'

'So, you are going to run your life around this little fella?'

'I am the dog father. He will be company for me, I will love it.'

'I am impressed by your commitment. There will be toilet training, remember.'

'You forget, I have done it all before with the boys. This will be much easier.'

They drove home with the new arrival. AP would cement their relationship. Patrick must want them to have a future together. The three of them.

CHAPTER FOURTEEN

Patrick woke up early and left shortly after for his appointment. The boys were back, for a few days; they had been on dog duty. Geoff was aware that Leona had stayed the night. He had heard his father leave the house and drive away. Geoff left his room with a towel wrapped around his waist. Leona came out of the bathroom, still tired and dreamy. Their eyes locked. He was drawn to Leona; he fancied her so much. They stood, eyes fixed on each other, but said nothing.

 She reached for his hand and led him into his father's bedroom. Without saying a word, she stretched out on the bed. Her long red hair sprayed around her delicate, pale face. The room was dark and still. He closed the door behind him. Gently, he pulled back the duvet, dropped the towel from his waist, and slipped into bed beside her. Leona looked so peaceful. She moved a little and sighed, her eyes closed. He leaned over her and began to kiss her. He brushed her neck with his lips; she smiled at the sensation. He moved to her collarbone, down to her chest and licked her smooth white flesh. He could smell her perfume mixed with a musky smell of woman – it was intoxicating. He pressed his body against hers and lightly stroked her inner thighs. She sighed and began to moan with pleasure. He caressed and stimulated her passions further. She opened her legs a little more and he wasted no time and pushed himself inside her. Leona opened her eyes slightly, her body in ecstasy. Geoff's heart beat like a drum as he plunged deeper within her, faster and faster.

It was over, done. The stillness, and silence, was all that remained. Geoff got out of bed, picked up the towel and left the room.

* * *

Leona returned home to Cheshire. She and Martin were now in separate rooms and that suited her. The following morning, after Martin left for a game of golf, Leona went downstairs, still high and turned on by what had happened between her and Patrick's son. It was a marvellous experience, but one she should not consider experiencing again. She collected the mail. Another small white envelope waited for her. This was the third letter she had received. It scared her; she was still unsure if Martin was behind them. The sender threatened to kill her unless she got out of Patrick's life. She would have to call him.

* * *

Patrick sounded frustrated. 'I don't believe this is happening.'

'I told you when I received the first letter. The second one made me feel weird. This third letter is more sinister. What if Martin had opened it? How would I have explained and talked my way out of it? It has a London postmark, for God's sake.'

'Calm down, there must be a simple explanation.'

'It's not you that's being threatened. What about your little friend at the theatre?'

'What little friend?'

'Bloody Justin. He hates me and adores you.'

'Justin hates everyone I enjoy being with. It's the way he is. If it makes you feel safer, I will check it out.'

Leona sensed she was getting on his nerves with her worries. She took a deep breath to calm herself down.

'Thank you, darling.'

'It could be Martin. He could have sent the letters to scare you, to stop our affair.'

'He knows nothing about us.'

'How can you be sure?'

'It's not his style – he would just blurt it out.'

* * *

The following Friday, Leona made a rush visit to see Patrick for a night of passion. It was worth it, just to be with him. He had become more demanding; she tolerated his behaviour rather than lose him. Leona never scared easily but she had become wary of Patrick's behaviour. She reassured herself that what she and Patrick had between them was a game, although she had to admit he had changed. He had started to frighten her. He took from her and gave back nothing.

* * *

Patrick left the house early, leaving Leona on her own to pack her stuff and leave. Leona felt alone, abandoned, and old. The taxi was due in half an hour. She went upstairs to collect her bag. She heard the front door open, followed by footsteps up the stairs. Tense, she turned around and was momentarily relieved as she recognised who it was. There was an unusual look in his eyes.

'What are you doing back here?' she asked nervously.

'Come back for more, have you?'

CHAPTER FIFTEEN

A week later.

'God, I am dying.' He woke up on the bedroom floor, sick to his stomach. As he attempted to move his arm, he sent a half bottle of vodka across the floor.

'I have to put an end to this.' His body weight pulled him back to the ground as he descended into a black abyss.

He was jolted from his slumber by the doorbell. As he rubbed his face, he noticed he had not shaved in days. Someone rang the doorbell, and kept their finger on it – the continuous shrill pierced his ears. Heavy, from sleep and a hangover, he dragged himself to his feet.

'Who the hell can it be?'

A dreaded, familiar depression had set in. He wanted to be alone, in the comfort of his own bed, to hibernate under the protection of the soft, voluminous duvet.

'Go away,' he bellowed. The irritating bell chimed on; he staggered down the stairs.

'Darling, it's me, let me in.'

Leona pushed past him and breezed along the hallway into the living room.

'You look like death.'

He closed the door against the chill of the night and mumbled, 'I can do without this.'

Wearily, he joined Leona, who mixed them both a gin and tonic.

'Not for me, Leona.' He plunged heavily into the armchair.

'You, saying no to a drink?'

He rubbed his head. 'This isn't a good time. What are you doing here?'

'I told you I would come down if Martin was away.'

'Like I said, it's not a good time.' He craved solitude.

'Tough, I'm here.' She picked up her bag and walked to the stairway.

'Where are you going?'

'To take my bag upstairs.'

'Like hell you are. I need to be alone – that means on my own.'

He moved swiftly and blocked her from going up the stairs.

'What the hell am I supposed to do?'

'Check in to a hotel.'

Leona was determined to stay.

'Better still, piss off back to where you came from, back to Martin, be a good wife.'

'I am staying right here.' She dropped her bag onto the floor.

His patience deserted him. 'What we had is over.'

'Why? We are good together, two of a kind.'

'It's finished. There is no easy way to end this, just get your things and go.' At the end of his tether, he stomped back to the living room.

'No way, who is she?'

'Who is who?' He inhaled to calm himself.

'The woman you are dumping me for. It all fits into place now. The hate mail… she sent them.'

'Don't be stupid.' His head thudded and he felt confused. 'I don't know who sent the letters. I don't care whether you believe me or not, but believe this: we are history.'

'I'm not about to conveniently disappear.'

He had to get rid of her. 'What about your husband?'

'Don't use Martin as leverage to be rid of me. Tell Martin everything. I don't care, I only want you.'

'I don't want you.'

'I will leave Martin. I will leave him right now. I will call him.' She was frantic; he had never seen her like this.

'Leona, go back to your husband. Stick with Martin. It's your best bet.'

'You don't mean that.'

'I don't want you. Now, get your coat and belongings and go.' He picked up her coat and threw it at her. Any chink in his armour would give her the opportunity to wriggle her way back into his life and into his head. He wasn't about to give her any false hope that this relationship could be rekindled.

'You bastard. I will get you back for this.' She walked to the door. 'Just tell me how long you have been seeing her?'

He decided to come clean. 'A few months. You and I were washed up before I met her.'

'Well, thanks for telling me.' Her face contorted. 'By the way, stud. You ceased to satisfy me a long time ago, too. Around the time I started screwing your son.'

Dazed, he tried to speak, but he was unable to formulate the words. Instead, they froze in his mouth and his jaw dropped.

'Lost for words. Don't you want to know which son it was?'

He was unable to move, as he tried to take in what she had said.

'Was it Matthew? I think it was him, or was it Geoff?' She put on her coat and picked up her bag. 'I will destroy you, or maybe I will destroy your son.'

'You ever go near either of my boys, I will kill you.'

'That sounds like the Patrick I have come to know and hate. Keep looking over your shoulder. You have added one more enemy to that very long list.'

* * *

Annette answered the phone. It was Patrick.

'I need you, Annette. Move in with me.'

'When did you decide this?'

'Just now.'

Annette was flattered and excited. She started babbling about the logistics of moving to London.

'One other thing – will you marry me?'

All her Christmases had come at once. Without hesitation, she accepted his proposal. She would marry him.

'Shall I give in my notice at work? I could be living with you permanently within a month.'

'Er, maybe…'

'You sound very tired.'

'Yes… er…'

'I can't understand what you are saying. Patrick, Patrick.'

He had fallen asleep. She could hear him snoring.

Annette was due to move in that week. Patrick had a cleaning agency blitz the house. He wanted to make a fresh start. He prayed Leona would keep away.

Within the past twenty-four hours she had left ten abusive messages. She had threatened to tell Martin everything. She was implying Martin was some kind of axe murderer. Patrick had no intention of returning her calls. He would take his chance with the wronged husband if need be.

In her last message, she said she had received another poison pen letter. She was clearly shaken up – the fear was audible in her voice. She said she would show the letters to the police. Was she bluffing? For a brief moment he wondered if one of his sons had sent the letters, then dismissed the idea. Whichever son had been intimate with Leona, neither would be in love with her. They would hardly be jealous of their father.

Justin came to mind. He must tell Justin it was all over with Leona, just in case he had anything to do with the letters. Now he and Leona were through, the letters should stop. Problem solved. Patrick was going straight. He was going to be monogamous – his bloody life depended on it. Annette was to be his salvation.

* * *

Annette arrived at Euston station, with her worldly belongings in two suitcases. Patrick was overjoyed to see her; he had been so lonely and depressed recently. Deep inside, he felt a little sorry for her. He would be good to her; he would try not to destroy her sense of decency. She deserved better than him, but he was not about to do the honourable thing and set her free. He needed her in his life. She would do anything for him; he also knew her naivety would mean she'd easily fall prey to his cunning nature. He would try to be good to her.

Two weeks down the line, they had fallen into a routine.

Annette had never felt comfortable at the house when alone and now was no different. She still felt uneasy. There was a presence, more so in certain rooms. They still never used the room at the front of the house. It remained the most cold and austere.

The boys came home occasionally, for money and to raid the fridge, use the shower and stay the night when it suited them. They still made her feel she was invading their space, their mother's territory. She desperately wanted them to like and accept her but knew this was a lot to expect. They probably viewed her as a passing fancy. Geoff was still rude but less aggressive. Matthew was the approachable one, even though he made no real effort to engage with her.

Geoff could withdraw and behave in a peculiar manner when it suited him.

Then again, they were young and had been cast adrift. Both were incredibly rude to their father, who never responded or called them to account for their bad behaviour. He just shrugged it off, as if he somehow deserved it. However, the boys were good to AP, which demonstrated a kind side to their personality.

* * *

Annette's mother rang.

'Have you settled in?'

'Yes, I've inherited your love of gardening. I have spent the past hour pulling up weeds. I've cut down the tall, over-grown foliage – things are taking shape. AP is my constant companion; you will love him when you meet him. He scampers around and generally disrupts my organised garden plan – he kicked over the black bin bags full of garden waste, chasing his tail until he was dizzy.'

'He sounds lovely.'

'His sense of fun and love of life rubs off on me. He fills my heart with joy.'

'That's good to hear.'

Annette gabbled on to fill any gaps that might give her mother the opportunity to tell her what a big mistake she had made, leaving Harts Gallery.

'The garden and AP are my sanctuary. All I need now is a small garden shed, where we can shelter from the rain, or sit in the shade from the sun.'

'Have you thought about going back to work?'

'I've considered it. I'll leave it a month or so before I start to look at what's available.'

'Don't throw all your options away, in case things don't work out.'

'Mum, it will work out. We are devoted to each other. We have AP, he belongs to both of us. We are a couple.'

'Have you got an engagement ring yet?'

'Not yet.'

'He needs to commit to you. The ring is a start.'

'He will get round to it. I need to get back in the garden before it rains. Thanks for the call. Bye, Mum.'

CHAPTER SIXTEEN

Leona took a cigarette and lit it with her special gold lighter. It had been a gift from Patrick, the only gift he had ever given her in the early days of their liaison. She recalled how he had lit her cigarette with the lighter and pushed it into her hand and said something corny like 'It will set you alight, as I do.'

She flung the lighter across the room and paced up and down, drawing heavily on the cigarette. Everything she enjoyed reminded her of him.

A gin and tonic calmed her down. She came up with a plan to hire a small, inconspicuous car, paid for with cash. She would drive to London, daily if necessary, and observe what was happening at Patrick's Hampstead home.

* * *

On Tuesday morning, after Martin had left for work, she packed a light lunch and a bottle of water, locked up the house and set off for London to begin her surveillance. Because of heavy traffic and road works she arrived at her destination late, one o'clock. She parked up at the corner of the adjoining road and waited. The car she had hired was a white Ford Escort, common and unnoticeable. There was a time she wouldn't have been seen dead in it. An hour and nothing had happened. She wound down the window and lit a cigarette. Tired and irritated, she accepted that surveillance and speeding around in a Ford Escort was no longer an option after today.

At two fifteen, a car pulled up outside the house. Leona got out of her car for a better look. It was bloody Justin. She cursed under her breath. Patrick came out of the house and got into the car. Then they were gone.

Leona took a deep breath and exhaled slowly. What now? She wondered if one of his sons might be home. Not sure which one she had slept with. She hadn't seen him since their last liaison. He might be pleased to see her. Invite her in. Once in the house, she could take it from there. Patrick would probably not be back for hours.

She smoothed down her dress and made her way towards the house. It was quiet. She walked up the path to the door; her footsteps echoed. Leona hammered heavily on the door, four times. She heard a dog bark from inside and saw a shadowy figure through the pane of coloured glass. Damn, it was a woman, perhaps a girlfriend of one of the boys. She could always persuade him to get rid of her for the afternoon. Leona still believed she had animal magnetism, even if Patrick resisted.

The door opened.

'Yes.' The woman was five or ten years her junior, attractive but not sexy, no dress sense and from the look of her not very worldly. 'May I help you?'

'I'm a friend of the family. Are the boys in?'

'The boys are away.'

'If the boys are away, why are you here?'

'I'm sorry, I don't understand.'

'You are one of their girlfriends?'

She laughed. 'Hardly, but I am flattered that you think I am one of their contemporaries.'

'Who are you?'

'I live here, with Patrick.' The woman hadn't quite registered the situation. 'Where are my manners – Annette Preston, Patrick's other half. Who are you?'

Patrick had told Leona there was someone else; she had never expected her to be so much younger than herself and never thought he would move her in.

Leona felt the blood drain from her face. She turned on her heels and ran across the road.

'Excuse me. Do you want to leave a message?' Annette called after her.

She trembled as she fumbled to put the key in the car door. Once in the car, she sped off down the road, not knowing where to go or what to do. A short time later, she pulled up outside Highgate Cemetery.

Leona took herself on a tour of the great and the good. Highgate Cemetery was full of history and makers of history.

There was a waiting list to be buried there. She smiled. She would only get admission whilst on this side of the ground. Her tour began on the newer side of the cemetery. By the perimeter was the grave of Sir Ralph Richardson, a great actor of his time. She recalled one of his great films, *The Heiress*, which she saw as a child. Sir Ralph was cast as the father who blamed his plain, shy daughter for the death of his wife in childbirth. He convinced her that no man would ever love her for herself, only for her inheritance. His daughter started life as a naïve, gullible, trusting young woman and ended up unmarried, alone, and bitter. Leona knew only too well that if you are told often enough that you are bad and unworthy, you start to believe it.

She walked deeper into the old side of the cemetery, amongst the catacombs where generations of families had been buried. With age, the stone had crumbled, the exterior walls had disintegrated. It was possible to peer into the dark, gloomy interior, not a place where she would want to spend eternity.

On the east side was the grave of Karl Marx, a bust of the man above the grave. All these influential people, who still impacted on the lives of people today and probably always would. Not that she would leave any lasting mark on the world. A short modelling career doesn't hack it amongst these giants. Jolted from her private thoughts, she saw a Rastafarian man swagger towards her. He looked stoned, as he began to weave along the path. She was depleted of energy and the sight of him, as he got closer, unsettled her. Alone and vulnerable, she made haste to the car. Nauseous, she just wanted to get home.

* * *

Annette heard the car pull up. Patrick was home. She was happy in the knowledge she was to be Mrs Clarke. AP enthusiastically jumped all over Patrick. Their nuclear family was coming together nicely.

'I love you,' Annette said.

'What?' Preoccupied, he rummaged through a cupboard, AP playfully getting in his way.

'I said I love you.'

'I thought that's what you said.' He smiled. 'You look happy. Have you had a good afternoon?'

'A lovely day, thank you. I was in the garden for hours with AP. We need to get a garden shed for the garden tools, and somewhere for us to sit when it rains.'

'That can be arranged.'

'Oh, we had a visitor. A woman called shortly after you left with Justin. She was of the opinion I was the girlfriend of one of the boys.'

Patrick stopped what he was doing. 'A woman, you say.'

'Yes, said she was a friend of the family.'

'Who was she?'

'She didn't say. She asked who I was, I told her that I lived here with you, she looked at me strangely, and walked away.'

'You told a complete stranger who you were and your status?'

'She said she was a friend of the family.' Annette hovered around Patrick as she waited for an explanation.

'She could be anybody and you blabbed our business. I sometimes wonder.'

'What do you mean by you sometimes wonder?'

He was frowning. 'Never mind that. You told her we lived together?'

'So, what if I did? We do. It's not a secret.' Annette sensed he knew this woman; he was so uptight. 'She was tall, beautiful, dressed in expensive clothes. Does that description match anyone you know?'

'No. Probably a fan.'

'She asked about the boys.'

'It's no secret I have two sons. She must be a stage groupie.'

He returned his attention to the cupboard. The contents tumbled out. 'Damn.' He ran his hands through his hair.

'Are you sure you don't know who she is?' Annette's joy drained away.

'Positive. She could be a journalist. Have you seen a set of Tupperware? Should be in this cupboard.'

'A journalist would have introduced herself.'

'Would you please take AP outside? I can't find a thing with him jumping all over me.'

* * *

Leona arrived home at nine o'clock after a horrendous journey back north. Weary, she parked the Ford Escort two streets away and walked to the house. The lights were on. Martin was home before her. What should she say? *Oh, stuff it.* She had had enough of being answerable to him. *He's not my bloody keeper.*

Martin turned to look at her as she entered the hallway, a pious expression on his face.

'Hi, I didn't expect you home yet.' She threw her bag on the sofa.

He didn't answer.

'I'm going to have a shower and have an early night.' She walked towards the stairs.

'Come back here.'

'What?'

'Get back here.'

Leona walked to the sofa and kicked off her shoes; she sat down and massaged her foot.

'Where have you been?'

'I beg your pardon?'

'Just answer the question.'

She wracked her brains trying to think of something plausible to say. She was so weary, nothing came to mind, so she tried to front it out. 'I've been out.'

'I know, but where?'

'I went to see a friend.'

'Anyone I know?'

'No.'

'You are going to have to do better than that.'

'Martin, what has got into you?'

'Just answer the question – honestly, if that's possible.'

'I met up with a friend from the health club I used to go to.'

'Where does this friend live?'

'I can't quite remember the address. I took a taxi. It's not that far away.'

'You took a taxi?' He walked towards the sofa, towering over her.

'Yes,' she said.

'It must have cost a lot, a journey to London in a taxi.'

Leona froze. 'What do you mean, a taxi to London?'

'I will ask the questions.'

She would have to admit where she had been. 'Okay, I have been to London.'

'Not by taxi?' He grabbed her arm and dragged her onto her feet.

'No, I went by train.'

His hand struck the side of her face; she fell to the floor.

'Liar.'

Martin had a volatile side but he had never struck her before.

He grabbed her hair and pulled her towards him. In a frenzy, he kicked her mercilessly. He didn't stop until he was too exhausted to continue the assault. Leona lay motionless, her face and mouth bled onto the carpet, her body sore and weak. He knelt down beside her.

'I know everything. You couldn't keep away from him?' He got to his feet.

Leona winced, anticipating another kick.

'You thought you could cheat on me? Outsmart me? I know what you've been up to.'

Leona lay still, unable to speak or cry.

Martin left the room. She heard the back door close. The car started up. It purred its way into the distance. Relieved, she tried to get up from the floor, as she gasped in pain. She rolled onto all fours, crawled slowly to the stairs and took one stair at a time. She reached the bathroom door. She collapsed.

* * *

Leona woke in a haze. Events came back to her bit by bit. A whirling sound, louder and louder – she became conscious of running water. Then it stopped. Unsure of where she was, she managed to open one eye, just as Martin stepped over her. She heard him go downstairs and leave the house.

It was morning. She had spent the night on the bathroom floor. Carpet fibres stuck to her face, which was covered in dried, crusted blood. She raised her elbows onto the lavatory seat and tried to lift herself to her feet. In agony, she unfolded her body as much as she could and leaned against the wall for support. Her ribs ached. She gripped the side of the wash basin, terrified of what she would see in the mirror. She braced herself, counted to three, and looked up.

How did she get here?

As she sat on the toilet seat, the open window behind her allowed her to breathe in the morning air. The last twenty-four hours had been traumatic. Whatever she and Martin had had was gone forever. He had used her as a punch bag. You can never come back from that.

Martin arrived at the office. He owned a large company that produced and supplied the components required to build technical equipment – this was the future.

'Harry, good to see you.'

'You look tense, everything okay?'

Harry was a loyal member of the team; Martin had confided in him. He followed Martin into his office.

'She got back late from London.'

'She went again. After what you said?'

'She's mad about him. I wish he felt the same.'

'He might?'

'Why would he take her on when he gets what he wants without the commitment?'

'I don't know what to say.' Harry looked uncomfortable.

'I was so disappointed when she turned up last night. I prayed she'd not come back. I was angry that he had sent her back to me.'

'Separate? File for divorce?'

'Oh, she'd love that. If I divorce her, she'll get half of all I have. I am lumbered with her.'

'What's the alternative?'

'I'm going to drive her away. I've stopped her money, locked her car in the garage. When she came through that door last night, after he had had her, I snapped. They're taking me for a bloody fool.'

Harry shuffled his feet.

'I lost it.'

Harry, with a worried expression, asked, 'Is she okay?'

'Don't worry, she's still alive. What the hell is it going to take to be rid of her?'

* * *

Leona considered calling her sister, though they had not spoken in five years.

The fair-weather friends would gloat if they knew her predicament. She could not contact Belinda again, after how she had belittled her, certainly not with a face like this. Her heart lurched at the thought of life without her credit card. All that remained was an all-consuming passion for Patrick. She had to get him back, at any price. That woman, Annette Preston, was cohabiting with her man.

Annette Preston would have to go.

CHAPTER SEVENTEEN

The alarm went off at eight o'clock. Patrick rolled over, hit the switch and dozed off again. Annette stayed awake. She knew he would need a nudge in five minutes. She needed to speak to Patrick, about the odd, spooky things that occurred in the house. She could well imagine his response. It would set the day off to a bad start, but it had to be done or it would drive her nuts.

Whilst Patrick showered and dressed, she considered how to approach the subject.

He joined her in the kitchen; she offered him a coffee.

'I'll get the newspaper. It's just been delivered.'

He looked up at her and raised his eyebrows as if he sensed she was about to raise something.

'I know this might sound ridiculous, but…'

He grunted. She took a deep breath.

'I think the house is haunted.' She looked away.

He continued leafing through his paper.

'I said, I think the house is haunted.' Annette stepped from one foot to another.

'Don't be ridiculous.'

'It's not my imagination. Things have happened.'

'Such as?'

'I leave the lights on and they are switched off when I return.'

'It's an energy-saving ghost?'

'Lights flash on and off around the house.'

'Ludicrous. There is a good explanation for lights flickering – power surges, for example.'

'Other things have happened. Stuff moves around the kitchen. One minute it is there, then it's gone.'

'What stuff?'

'The sugar bowl was on the table. I went back into the kitchen; it had gone. I checked every cupboard. Later, it was back on the table.'

'Annette, I have a busy day ahead. I can't deal with this now. Go for a long walk with the dog, clear your head and relax. There is no pressure on you here. It has been a big upheaval, the move and having to adjust to a new lifestyle. Just take it easy.'

He took off his spectacles, folded the newspaper, and kissed her on the forehead. 'See you later.'

She forced a weak smile and nodded.

Numerous things had happened in the house. What some people might refer to as supernatural occurrences. If she mentioned it again, he would become hostile and distant. Did Patrick not sense a presence? Was she being insensitive, to talk of an unfriendly spirit?

After a morning walk with AP, she took a drink and magazine into the living room and snuggled into Patrick's comfy armchair.

The magazine feature was about women who marry men with a family. Three women had been interviewed. Patrick was so bohemian and timeless. He was not your usual dad.

Excruciating pain seared across the back of her head. Her fingers touched her scalp, and she felt the sticky, wetness of blood. She jumped out of the chair and saw what had struck her – the painting she had put up a few days ago. The frame had split, and the glass had shattered. Blood oozed. Panicked, she rang Patrick at work.

'Come home now, please.'

'What's happened?'

'The bloody painting fell on my head and I can't stop the blood flow.' She burst into hysterical sobs.

'I told you not to put the painting up. Calm down, it was an accident. I will be home in an hour.'

Then she said the very thing she knew would aggravate and anger him. 'Do you think Victoria did this? Is she behind what is going on in this house?'

* * *

Patrick was livid. His stomach churned and his heart was heavy with pain.

'Stop this nonsense. Go to the hospital or call an ambulance if the wound is so bad.'

''Patrick, I am terrified.'

'Just do it.' He slammed down the telephone. His hands shook, his breath rapid. What had got into her? He couldn't cope with this hysteria. Why did women, his women, drive him mad? He was being driven to an early grave.

The watercolour painting had been Victoria's. Annette had found it under the stairs and had persuaded him to put it up.

He thought about his wife, Victoria. His guilt overwhelmed him. It tore at his soul without mercy. Why did she have to die? Why could it not have been him? He would have to tell Annette the full story. He couldn't put it off any longer.

* * *

Annette returned from the casualty department. She had needed a couple of stitches. Because of her state of distress, she had been given a tranquilliser. She lay on the sofa, in a daze, relaxed and detached. How good that felt.

* * *

Patrick arrived home, looking weary and broken. She noticed how old he looked. He threw off his coat and sat by her. 'Are you okay?'

'Yes. I needed a couple of stitches, but I'm fine.'

Annette lay back against a cushion. He took her hand in his.

'I'm sorry I didn't come home straight away when you called. What you said about Victoria, it paralysed me.'

'I'm sorry too. It must have sounded crazy.'

'No need to apologise. I chose not to discuss Victoria's death with you, because I have spent years trying to block it out. I try, but it never goes away.' He paused.

'I was the cause of her death. I was drunk at the wheel of the car. I am so ashamed.'

'What happened?'

'We hit a tree. I don't remember a thing. I was out of it. I was charged with causing death by reckless driving, much to the dismay of Victoria's parents. I got a suspended sentence, suspended for two years. The court's leniency was due to my having the boys to raise. They had lost their mother – to lose their father, too? The boys will never forgive me. Why should they? I will never forgive myself.'

94

Annette had never witnessed such despair and sorrow. She also had a deep sense of jealousy, for the woman he had made vows to, who he had twin boys with, the woman he killed.

'Did Victoria love you?'

He looked up, surprised by her question. 'Once upon a time, yes she did.'

'Did she love you before the accident?'

'I don't think so.'

'Would she forgive me for loving you? Would she haunt me?'

'If you had asked me yesterday, I would have said no. But she haunts me every minute of every day since the blasted accident. I deserve it, I killed her.' He gazed at the floor.

'It was an accident.'

'I was at the wheel. I was stoned. We had argued. She wanted a divorce, she wanted me out of her life. I couldn't bear it; I wasn't going to let her leave me.

'She had already taken the boys to live with her parents. I could handle that. I knew where she and the boys were, and it allowed me to do my own thing. But a divorce? I didn't want her out of my life completely. I was consumed with fear. I had to keep her in my life. I had no concentration as I drove the car off the road and hit a tree. I remember the argument and then blackness. It haunts me. I robbed her of all she treasured. The boys lost their mother. Her parents lost their only daughter. I caused all this loss, pain and misery.'

'Haven't you paid enough?' Tears began to well in her eyes.

'I have had no peace since she died. I try to block it out with booze, drugs, and sex. A shrink told me I was subconsciously killing myself with excesses. Every morning I wake up to blackness and self-loathing. I never know if I will get through the day.'

'I am here now. I can support you.'

'Dearest Annette, I am already on borrowed time. No one can save me from myself.' He left the room and went upstairs. She heard the study door slam shut.

CHAPTER EIGHTEEN

It had all happened so suddenly. Screams, delusional ramblings. The ambulance took Patrick to a place of safety, where he was assessed by a psychiatrist. Then he was admitted to the Priory Hospital in Roehampton.

Unsure what to take, Annette decided on a bunch of pink and white roses. He wouldn't want grapes, and she wasn't about to take cigarettes, which no doubt he would have preferred. Certainly no alcohol was permitted – he had been on the five-day detoxification programme.

His system was free of alcohol – Librium assisted with the withdrawal symptoms. There had been no visitors during the detox period; he had been delirious. She was pleased the psychiatrist had persuaded him to remain in hospital for a further three weeks, where he would participate in individual and group therapy.

Annette arrived at the Priory reception. Patrick was in unit one. The nurse told her he was in the day room. As she approached the glass doors, she wondered what state he would be in. Half expecting him to be a jabbering idiot, she was pleased to see him sitting at a table with a group of people playing cards. What a relief – he looked quite normal. Patrick gave a roar of jubilation; he had won the game.

'Patrick.'

'Annette. I hope you are here to take me out of this place?'

One of the players offered Annette his seat and ambled away.

'You can't just come home. The consultant will have to see you before you are discharged.'

'I can leave when I bloody well like. I wasn't sectioned.'

'Don't do anything rash,' she urged. 'You're doing really well.'

'I don't want the press to know I am in here. I've already signed about ten autographs.'

'I understand.'

'I wasn't sectioned?'

'No, but you did lose it.'

Patrick raised his hand to silence her. 'I don't want the details, not yet. Does anyone know I am here? The boys?'

'No, no one.'

'So, you haven't told anyone?'

'No. I brought you these.' She offered him the flowers.

Patrick lit a cigarette. 'Hey, Mary, come over here.'

A middle-aged woman in a dressing gown came over.

'Mary, these are for you.' The woman took the flowers and smiled; she walked away.

'Thanks for the flowers. It was a nice thought.'

'You're welcome.'

'They will give Mary more pleasure than me. I'm on some sedative, strictly no booze. Not that I need alcohol, I feel stoned most of the time.'

He lowered his voice. 'I am glad you didn't visit before today. I was delusional for the first few days, paranoid, panicking, seeing crazy things, shouting, sweating, shaking all over – not a pretty sight. I've still got the shakes, but the medication helps.' He held out a trembling hand.

'I love you.' She squeezed his hand.

'I know you do. God knows why. Why didn't you tell the boys?'

'I didn't have the energy to track them down.'

'So, you have told absolutely no one? How are you, alone in the house at night? Are you able to sleep? I know the house spooks you and what with me going off my head…'

She took his hand in hers. 'Slow down. I have AP on the bed with me and I keep a lamp on all night. Darling, you have been under a lot of pressure. I don't want to add to it. Don't worry about me.'

'You could check into a hotel?'

'What about AP?'

'Ring Matthew. He's a good boy, he would look after AP.'

'Don't worry, I am fine. As long as you are in here and getting the help you need, I can manage being home alone.'

'I've an appointment with the psychiatrist next week. I will be able to update you then. I have agreed to stay here another three weeks, to keep them happy. I suppose I can sit it out. You will have to let a few people know where I am. Make an excuse to anyone else. I will put a list together of who should be told.'

'I think you have made the right decision staying here for a few more weeks.'

'I'll be good as new.' He put out his cigarette and reached out to hug her. 'I am tired. I think I'll have a nap. You get yourself home to AP.'

'Shall I visit tomorrow?'

'Some of the sessions take place in the evenings. Ring reception first, no point travelling all this way for nothing.'

Annette hesitated.

'Patrick, I think I will apply for a job. I can't keep living off you.'

'Nonsense, I don't see it that way. I need you at home.'

'Why?'

'I like to know you are there. Once we are married and start a family, you will be busy.'

'I don't want children straight away.'

'Of course you do. You're not getting any younger and I'm certainly not. A couple of children is what we need. I want to start again.'

She reached the doorway. She had to say it. 'I feel isolated. I've even considered giving Liz a call.'

That got his attention. A stern expression crossed his face.

'But I haven't.'

'Annette, you don't need anyone. We have each other, I don't want to share you.' He beckoned her over. He kissed her, which silenced her protests.

'I need to rest, you understand. Join me for an early dinner tomorrow – join me every day for dinner. They don't mind family in the hospital restaurant, at a charge of course. That will stop you feeling isolated.'

By the time Annette arrived home the best of the day was over. As she approached the house, she saw the lights were on; Matt or Geoff must be home.

Tired, she called out to see who was around.

'Hello.'

No one in the living room. She went upstairs. All the doors to the rooms were open, all the lights had been left on. She turned off the lights in each room one by one. There was no one around. She thought she heard mumbles downstairs; it became louder. Back downstairs she checked out the kitchen and sighed with relief – the radio was on. AP scratched at the back door. The poor boy must have been put outside and then forgotten about. She would have a serious chat with Geoff and Matthew. They should never leave AP locked outside.

Annette fed a hungry AP, gave him a treat and then took him for a short walk.

A neighbour greeted her. 'Excuse me. I saw an ambulance outside your house the other day. Is everything all right?'

'Yes. Thank you.'

'I live two doors down, if you need anything.'

'That is very kind.'

Annette continued the walk. AP pulled on the lead. He wanted a run, but a walk would have to do.

The neighbours kept themselves to themselves as a rule. They all must know Patrick was an actor. She wasn't about to divulge their private details to anyone, no matter how well meaning.

Annette retired to bed with her trusted friend AP by her side. She lay rigid and contemplated sleeping downstairs. The hours ticked by. She listened out for every tiny sound.

Patrick was propped up in his bed as he scoured the daily newspapers that had been delivered to the unit. He wanted to be reassured no one had tipped off the press. There was a rap on the door.

'Come in,' he shouted.

It was a male nurse. 'Morning, Patrick, you have a visitor. It's highly irregular to allow visitors on the unit outside of visiting hours, but he said he was a good friend and had travelled some distance.'

'Who is it?'

'Justin Sharp.'

'Oh, let him in.'

'Ten minutes, tops. Your morning group session starts at nine thirty, and you need to have breakfast.'

'Don't worry, I will be on time.'

Justin rushed in.

'Justin, how on earth did you know I was here?'

'I have been trying to get in touch with you to no avail, so I went round to yours and she said you were away. I knew that wasn't true as you never go anywhere. So, I followed her here yesterday.'

'You followed her. Very Sherlock Holmes.'

'I wanted to observe her, to see what she has that I don't.'

'I thought that would be bloody obvious.'

'I wanted to weigh up the competition. I wanted to catch her out, see if she was having an affair.'

'Annette doesn't have time for affairs. She has me.'

'Stop boasting. She is far too dull for any hanky-panky, unlike that dreadful tart, Leona.'

'Oh, Justin, your jealousy has become tiresome.'

Justin pulled up a chair. 'As I said, I followed her, she led me here. Never in a million years would I have guessed you would be in a place like this.'

'A nut house – go on, say it.'

'I rang the Priory admissions, just to be sure you were in here. I said I was your son.'

'You are too old to be my son.'

'I was worried. I have never been on a psychiatric ward before.'

'Is that so.'

'I didn't mean to offend you.'

'Well, you did.'

'Sorry.'

* * *

In the early evening, Patrick joined the group. The speaker was in full flow.

'You can visit an AA meeting almost every day, all around the country and all around the world. You will always be welcomed. It is a fellowship, that will turn no one away. Groups of people being true to themselves. Freedom from addiction means you will stay alive, free of fear, paranoia, sickness of the body, mind and spirit.'

Patrick knew he had been sick for years and he was tired of it. He had been sick with addiction before the accident - the accident had simply accelerated his demise.

The group facilitator thanked the speaker.

'Are there any questions?'

A patient spoke. 'I have managed in here for three weeks without alcohol. Surely, when I go home, I can have the occasional drink, once a week with friends at the pub?'

'No, you can't. If you have a drink, you will want another. Each day you will need more and eventually you will become ill again, but worse than before.' The facilitator looked around. 'Yes, Derek?'

'My entire social life revolved around alcohol, at the pub, golf club, wine club. A drink at the end of the day to wind down, a treat, a celebration or commiseration. How do I manage my problem?'

'You say no to alcohol.'

'But how do I explain not drinking?'

'You tell them you have stopped or you do what most of you will have to do, change your social life. Find new interests and outlets, new friends, start a new chapter.'

'But I collect wine, I have a wine cellar, I'm in the wine club.'

'You won't be able to do any wine tasting. I cannot impress upon you enough, you will have to change your life, your friends, your interests. If you go back to the old life, you will become ill and you will lose everything – health, family, your life.'

Patrick raised his hand.

'Yes, Patrick.'

'I want to tell you guys here what the deal is. You have a choice: no alcohol and live a new life or continue drinking and inevitably die.

'Initially, alcohol is a friend, helps you to cope, relax, gives confidence, you lose your inhibitions, and it helps you sleep. Gradually, this friend turns into your master, a demon master. All the relief it gave you comes at a price. You must pay back with your health, your sanity. You have to drink more for less relief, until the relief lasts for minutes, whilst the drinking is constant.'

'Thank you. Patrick, you have a lot of insight.'

'I have been here before.'

CHAPTER NINETEEN

As expected, Martin threatened to sell Leona's Jaguar. He had put a stop on her credit card. He was determined to humiliate her, break her. Leona knew Martin's vengeful behaviour was in return for his bruised ego, rather than because of devastation over her infidelities. It wasn't a case of 'how dare she betray me' but 'how dare she think she could get away with it'. He owned her; she was bought and paid for.

Leona was unable to call Patrick from the house, so she walked to a telephone box. She was annoyed at having to walk, and because she was black and blue she had to wear dark glasses and a jacket with the hood up. The neighbours or old acquaintances must never see her like this. Fortunately, they were rarely seen out here in no man's land. The odd pleasantry was as far as communication went around here.

At least the public telephone boxes hadn't been vandalised or peed in.

The call went to answerphone. As she heard Patrick's voice, she became tearful.

'Patrick, it's me, Leona. I am sorry I threatened you. I need to see you. Martin found out about us. I didn't tell him, I swear. He is a vicious bastard.' The beeps started; she had run out of coins. The line went dead.

Reluctantly, she returned home, obsessed with Patrick and that woman, Annette. She imagined them in bed together, doing all the things she had done with Patrick. It was unbearable. A jealous rage coursed through her veins, so powerful she felt she would explode.

I will kill her. Patrick is mine. She took a piece of writing paper, jotted a message, put it in an envelope, addressed it and put a stamp on it. Then she went to the post box.

Annette woke up to AP's howls. The radio was on downstairs. One of the boys must have let themselves in. She got out of bed and stood at the top of the stairs. It was freezing. The coldness enveloped her. She shivered and rubbed her arms. She was just about to switch on the light when a force of energy from behind sent her headfirst down the stairs.

* * *

The next day, after lunch, Patrick went to his room. He rang Justin, to ask him to call at the house. He had tried to contact Annette, but it repeatedly went to answerphone. He hadn't seen Annette since her initial visit.

'All I get is the blasted answer machine.'

'Women,' Justin replied dismissively.

* * *

A knock at the door.

'Patrick, you have a visitor,' the nurse said.

'About time too – show her in.'

'It's a young man.'

Matthew entered the room. 'Hi, Dad.'

'Matthew, my boy. How did you know I was here?'

Matthew sat on the edge of Patrick's bed. 'Listen, Dad, I have something to tell you. Don't stress, everything will be fine.'

'What's happened?'

'I knew you were here when I played back the messages on the answer machine. You had left a message, that you were stuck at the Priory, why hadn't Annette visited.'

'And why hasn't she?'

'I went to the house. Fortunately, I had my key.'

'She isn't dead, is she?'

Matthew looked puzzled by his father's question. 'No, but she was unconscious. She had fallen down the stairs. I rang an ambulance. I went with her to the hospital. She has regained consciousness but is completely out of it.'

'You are a good lad, Matthew.'

'Why did you ask if she was dead?'

'I thought the worst. Thank goodness she is okay. Thank goodness you went round.'

Matthew looked scornfully at his father. 'Do you think you are being fair to Annette?'

'What do you mean?' Patrick lay back on the bed, propped up by two large pillows.

'She can't be happy stuck in our house on her own, you in here. You and your waifs and strays,' he said as he looked at Justin, who had just walked into the room.

'Don't you like her?'

'I don't know her. I suppose she is a step up from what you normally drag home.'

Justin turned crimson. Matthew's eyes fell to the floor. Patrick felt uncomfortable and vulnerable. He was completely sober for the first time in years. He so wished his son hadn't brought up his liaisons in front of Justin. Patrick could feel his face flush; he must be scarlet.

Matthew looked at him and started to splutter. 'I mean, she is younger than you.'

'Not that much. Does it bother you?'

'What do you have in common? What do you share that could guarantee a stable, lasting relationship?'

'What makes you think I want a stable, lasting relationship? Did I ever say it was a long-term arrangement?'

'You have asked her to marry you, for God's sake.'

Justin was beside himself. 'You have asked her to marry you? Why didn't you tell me?'

'It's none of your business.'

Justin was flabbergasted. Patrick ignored him and carried on.

'I want you to stay over at the house with Annette, when she is discharged from hospital.'

'Me?'

'I have to stay here for another three weeks. If I leave now, I will be no use to anyone. I would appreciate it if you would. I don't think it's safe for her to be alone.'

'She's got the dog,' Matthew said.

'I mean it. I need you to stay overnight.'

'Why should I?'

'It would give me peace of mind. I don't have much of that at present, as you can see.' Patrick raised his arms, helplessly. 'Matthew, strange things have been happening at the house, late at night.'

'First I've heard of it. Such as?'

'Odd things, noises and disturbances.'

'The house is haunted?' Matthew asked.

Patrick was irritated by Matthew's impertinence. 'Yes, I think it is.'

'So, it's all right for me to be in the bloody house, your own flesh and blood. Doesn't matter what happens to me.'

'I am sure you will be in no danger.'

'No, maybe I will get shoved down the stairs? What is this entity? Has Annette seen anything?'

Patrick lowered his voice. 'She has heard things and saw a shadowy figure upstairs.'

'She has seen a ghost?'

'It might sound strange but there is… I don't know.' He shook his head.

'You believe her?'

'I have sensed things too.' Patrick was uncomfortable; he looked down at the floor.

'What?'

'I thought I saw your mother.'

'How dare you, both of you. Do you really think my mother would stick around that house? She couldn't get away fast enough, she never wanted to go back there, and she certainly didn't want to see you again. No wonder you ended up in this place.'

Matthew jumped from the edge of the bed where he had been sitting. He almost knocked over Justin by the sheer force of his movement.

'I am sorry that I brought your mother into this, but you asked, and I told you.'

'How low will you stoop?'

'Matthew, I can't deal with this in my present state. I need to be left alone, to get well.'

'I will leave you alone all right, I will leave Annette alone too. I will not stay overnight to babysit a grown woman, who clearly has issues with my dead mother. Ask Geoff to stay.'

'No, I don't want him there.'

'Suit yourself.' Matthew left the room in a rage.

* * *

Leona was desperate. Patrick had not returned her calls, and Martin was impossible to live with. He had sacked the cleaner and expected her to do it. Life was meaningless without Patrick. Leona ran the vacuum cleaner through the house with a drink in her hand; it made the chores seem less demeaning. She was tormented with imagery of Patrick and Annette together. She plotted different ways to dispose of Annette – poison her, push her into oncoming traffic, run her over.

* * *

Matthew collected Annette from hospital. She was discharged with painkillers.

He assisted her into Patrick's battered BMW.

'Thank you, Matthew. Are we going straight home?'

'Yes, you need to rest.'

'Have you seen your father today?'

'Dad's fine. I promised him I would take you to visit him as soon as you are well enough.'

'I feel well. We could go later today.'

'Only if you rest. You need to get used to being at the house again.'

Annette thought how kind it was of Matthew to take care of her on behalf of his father. There was the potential for them to become friends, become a family.

'Dad insists I stay over with you, for the time being.'

'He did?' Relief swept over her.

'He thinks the house is haunted.'

'He does?' She leant her head on the head rest and took a deep breath.

'Yeh, crazy or what?'

'I think so too.' She glanced over at him.

'You do?'

'Things happen that can't be explained. There is a foreboding presence.'

'I'm going to be there. So, any spookiness will have me to deal with.'

Annette squeezed his hand.

Matthew pulled up outside the house and assisted Annette as she made her way inside.

'I will take your bag upstairs. You go and make yourself comfortable. I will make us both a hot drink.'

Annette sat on the sofa. Glancing around the room, she wondered if the ghost was watching her.

Matthew hurried downstairs and busied himself in the kitchen. He returned with a tray of tomato soup and sand-wiches and a pot of tea for two.

'You are so kind.'

'No problem. Dad would want me to take care of you. I actually enjoy doing it.'

Matthew remained at the house for the rest of the day and only when he was convinced Annette was well enough did he agree to take her to visit Patrick.

* * *

They arrived at the Priory at six o'clock.

'Darling.' Patrick's voice echoed around the room.

Annette rushed into his arms and he kissed her passionately. Matthew felt embarrassed and a little jealous. He had enjoyed caring for Annette – her dependence on him made him feel strong, important.

'I will leave you both to catch up. Dad, there is a letter for you, marked urgent.'

* * *

Patrick checked the postmark and put the letter in the drawer.

'Matthew said you insisted he stay over at the house and that you believe it's haunted.'

'I wouldn't go that far.'

'But. He said—'

'Hush.' He put his finger to his lips. 'I don't want you on your own. Has Matthew said anything about us?'

'No. Why?'

'No reason.'

Annette went to the bathroom. Patrick wondered if the letter was from Leona. No matter how much he tried to fight it, just the thought of her set off the familiar stirring that he only felt for her. He considered giving her a call. One last fling. He tore open the letter the way he would have torn open her blouse. He scanned the contents. The loo flushed, so he put the letter back in the drawer.

Annette's energy started to wane. Matthew could see she was exhausted.

'I think we should get you home.'

As Annette and Matthew were about to leave, Justin arrived with a bouquet of red roses. He pushed his way past them as if they didn't exist.

'How is the patient?' Justin and Patrick immediately engaged in conversation. Annette turned to Matthew and shrugged; their departure went unnoticed.

* * *

They arrived back at the house. Annette was on her reserve energy tank.

'I had arranged to meet with friends. I hoped you might join me, but I can see you are exhausted.'

'I will have to decline your kind offer. Please, you go. I have already taken up your day.'

'Will you be okay on your own?'

'Yes, what time will you be back?' She shivered but tried to sound casual.

'About midnight. I will get going – there are a couple of letters for you on the hallway table.' He grabbed them and attempted to throw them to her. They fluttered in the air and landed on the floor.

'Bye, see you later.' The door slammed shut.

Annette scooped up the letters and sat on the sofa. One of the envelopes bore a resemblance to the hate mail she had received previously. She swallowed hard. Should she open them now or wait until tomorrow?

She would wait until Matthew got home. So tired from the medication and the journey to see Patrick, she fell asleep.

CHAPTER TWENTY

Whilst Martin showered, Leona went downstairs and waited for the post to arrive; she had been doing this on a daily basis. It got her from one day to the next, a minuscule hope in her world of futility. At eight o'clock, the postman did his rounds. She collected the post and anxiously sifted through the mail. There were two letters addressed to her, both with a London postmark. She looked for Patrick's handwriting. She placed the rest of the mail on top of the bureau, for Martin, and then crept upstairs. She closed the door to her walk-in wardrobe behind her. It was from him. She tore open the letter. It was brief – it told of his stay in the Priory. She concluded that was why he had not been in touch earlier and why he hadn't returned her calls. The letter continued, 'I will contact you soon, I miss you, especially at bedtime.' Leona was euphoric. She knew it – she knew he couldn't live without her. Things were going to change. She would get away from Martin for good. Goodbye, Cheshire; hello, London.

Full of optimism, she opened the second letter. A photograph and a piece of paper fluttered to the floor. She was stunned at the image. It was a nude photograph of her. She put her hand to her mouth, to silence herself. She studied the photograph and recognised the bedding, the rich crimsons that contrasted with her naked, ivory skin. This was Patrick's bed – when was it taken?

The note read, 'Bitch, you are going to die. You were warned. Now pay the price.'

Utterly bewildered, she looked at the photo and then the note. It disturbed her. Amidst the madness, she couldn't help but admire her toned, slender body, its perfect proportions. The image was most complimentary, almost artistic.

She wondered if this was one of Patrick's little games. He must have taken the photograph of her on his bed. How careless of him to post both letters together. Then again, he was in the Priory, he might have got a bit confused, or maybe he wanted her to put two and two together, a covert message. She decided it was Patrick who had sent all the letters; his game playing knew no bounds. The bedroom door swung open; she quickly stuffed the letters and photo between a pile of jumpers.

'Don't forget, the Havers are our guests on Saturday evening.' He marched to the bedside cabinet and put on his Rolex watch.

'How could I forget the Havers?' she said sarcastically.

Chances are he will be entertaining them alone, she thought smugly.

* * *

Unfortunately, her hopes had not come to fruition. Two weeks on, she walked to the telephone box, on a quiet Sunday morning, and rang Patrick's number.

Patrick answered, his voice groggy.

'It's me.'

He sighed, unable to hide his disappointment. This angered her.

'Not interrupting anything, I hope?'

'No. What do you want?'

'Still with that woman?' She could no longer contain her jealousy.

'I am with no one.'

'Liar.' She was still aggressive, but she was relieved by his answer. 'What about Justin? Does she know about him?'

'Stop this.'

Leona wasn't getting the response she had anticipated and was disappointed. 'Touchy. So she doesn't know about Justin? Perhaps the tabloids would be interested. I need money, to get away and start again.'

He lowered his voice. 'I am warning you.'

'And I am warning you. Get rid of her before I do. We belong together.' She realised she sounded antagonistic; he would put the phone down if she continued in this manner. She changed tactics because there was something she needed to know.

'Did you send me the letters and the photograph? Just be honest and tell me, I won't be mad.'

'I haven't sent you anything.' He sounded dismissive.

'A photograph of me naked.'

'One of your other lovers probably sent it – who else have you slept with?'

'It was taken on your bed, you idiot.' Panic shrilled in her voice.

'Goodbye, Leona. Don't contact me again.'

'I need you. What about Martin? He is violent, I'm scared of him.'

'He will forgive you eventually, and quite honestly, it isn't my problem.'

Leona went on the attack. 'Are you still with her? Give her up or I will kill her. I mean it, I will kill her.'

'Goodbye.' He hung up. She tried to call him back; the engaged tone was all she got.

Patrick and Annette were together at the house. Geoff was at his university digs. Patrick disconnected the downstairs telephone, but left the one in his study, where there was an answering machine.

He would arrange for the downstairs phone to be available for outgoing calls only. Annette was afraid to go out alone. After the last message she had received, she instinctively knew there was something Patrick had not told her about the woman who had turned up on the doorstep. It unnerved her that Patrick now took the matter seriously. Was the person who made the calls also sending the letters? She knew Patrick had played the messages in his study. She had crept upstairs and listened in at the door that connected to the bedroom. The tone of the voice on the answering machine always sounded the same, although she couldn't make out the words. Patrick insisted he did not know the woman who had turned up at the house. Annette didn't buy it. He refused to involve the police.

He was doing his best to protect them both; she had to trust that is what he would do.

The constant phone calls came to an abrupt halt. Patrick began to relax.

CHAPTER TWENTY-ONE

On Thursday morning, at ten o'clock, the doorbell rang three times, followed by loud thuds on the door. Annette opened the door and was taken aback to be greeted by three police officers, one in uniform, two plain-clothed.

'Good morning. Is this the residence of Mr Patrick Clarke?'

'Yes, he isn't at home.' She knew something was desperately wrong.

'Could you tell us where we might find him?'

'The Old Vic theatre. Well, he is on his way there.'

'Thank you for your help, madam.'

'Excuse me – could you tell me what has happened?'

'We need Mr Clarke to assist us with our enquiries. Good day to you.'

Annette called the Old Vic, in an attempt to speak to Patrick before the police did. It just rang out.

* * *

At eight o'clock that evening Patrick walked through the door. He was visibly shaken.

'Did the police find you? What's going on?'

'I have come from the police station, they thought I might be able to help them.'

'With what?'

'I was told some disturbing news.'

'What?'

'Not now. I've been grilled at the station. I don't want to talk about it.'

'I demand to know what is going on – who was the woman who turned up at the house?'

'I'm a suspect in a murder inquiry. Now leave it.'

'Who is she?'

'I can't take much more of this mental bombardment and I refuse to be drawn into an argument.'

He took two bottles of Scotch from the drinks cabinet and went upstairs. Annette followed him, trying to get a response. He ignored her, went into his study and closed the door. She heard the key turn on the other side. He had locked himself in, locked her out.

* * *

He lay on the sofa, an empty bottle beside him. He picked up the big floral cushion and buried his face into it. He pressed it harder and harder, pulled it tighter and tighter, to block out any light, sight, or sound. His hands and face were sore from the sheer tension. Uncontrollable tears flooded from his eyes as he recalled the wretched manner in which he had behaved towards her. He had treated her like rubbish. His grief-stricken insides churned as he pined for her. Overwhelmed by grief, he hadn't the strength to fight it, to push it down. Instead, it surged forth, through every nerve and fibre of his being. It tore down the barriers, gorged on his very soul. He was unable to fight the pain anymore. He lay engulfed in agony.

* * *

A couple of hours later, the tears subsided, the pain had numbed. He rolled over and crawled to the second bottle of whisky, drank from the bottle, gulped, and savoured the burning liquid. It set a flame in his stomach. He wanted to die, so all the torment would stop.

He was devastated she had met with such a dreadful death. He was also relieved she was out of the way and unable to bother him again. No more hysteria and threats. Of course, he would rather she was happy somewhere far away, rather than dead. But she would never have gone away. This was the ideal solution to his problem. It was such a relief.

The whisky was working its magic; he lay back and closed his eyes. He imagined what Leona's last moments of life had been like. The predator would overpower her, the struggle, the fight… at what point did she realise she would never get away, as she fought hopelessly for her life? He concentrated hard. He pictured the fear in her eyes. He could see them – pupils dilated, pools of darkness. He held on to the image as she tried to scream. No, he decided no sound had emerged from her. Blows to her body, the body she so adored, blows to the head, indiscriminate strikes caved in her skull. Blood soaked into her long red beautiful hair. As she fell to the ground and gasped for breath, she must have turned to her attacker, her eyes pleading and asking why. Completely powerless and at his mercy. Patrick became aroused. A rope around her ivory neck, its roughness pierced her smooth skin. Leona's face pushed hard into the cold, wet soil as the noose tightened. She would have spluttered until the airway completely closed. Then, no struggle. The game was over.

He erupted, in a frenzy of ecstasy and revulsion.

CHAPTER TWENTY-TWO

Annette woke up, fully clothed, to loud thuds on the front and back doors. AP barked and ran downstairs. She sat bolt upright and tried to orientate herself, then pulled back the curtains and was horrified to see scores of journalists, reporters, cameras, even a whole television crew, all outside at the house. Their voices grew louder as they spotted her at the upstairs window. Flash bulbs blinded her for a few seconds, their faces swam before her eyes.

Annette hammered at the study door. 'Patrick, Patrick, we are surrounded by the press.'

She heard the study door open out on to the landing. He was off down the stairs. The telephone rang out in the study. Reporters banged on the downstairs window; it was mayhem. She held on to the stairway railing – her legs wobbled as she descended the stairs, then she began to shake violently. The noise from outside was unbearable. Copies of tabloid newspapers had been pushed through the letterbox. Patrick hammered nails into the front door.

'What are you doing?'

'I want to ensure those vipers can't push any more crap through the door. I've nailed down the letterbox.'

The landline began to ring.

'For fuck's sake disconnect the phone.'

She picked up a newspaper, one of many that had been pushed through the letterbox. On the front page was a photograph of a woman – it was the same woman who had been to the house. Angrily, she ran upstairs into Patrick's forbidden lair, the first time she had stepped foot in his study. It was usually locked and everyone in the household was forbidden to enter. It was full of stuff, things that must have belonged to Victoria, big bin bags and boxes piled high, stuffed with God knew what.

She wanted to burn the bloody lot of it. Annette started to scream. She ran to the wall and pounded it with her fists. She ran from the study, full of ghosts of the past, to deal with the ghosts of the present. Patrick had been having an affair with the woman who came to the house, the woman he had told her he didn't know. What had she got herself into? Patrick was connected to these deaths. The woman on the front pages of the newspapers had been brutally murdered; his wife was dead, mangled in a car wreckage; she herself had received death threats, which he had played down.

Leona was on the front of every newspaper the length and breadth of the country. Annette was scared. She no longer trusted him. She didn't know him anymore – had she ever known him?

Downstairs, he had closed all the curtains. The house was dark and gloomy, as if it was night-time except for the noise outside. She sat in the armchair and watched Patrick as he lay on the sofa; he stared up at the ceiling. No longer prepared to tiptoe around his moods, she spoke calmly and in a measured tone.

'The woman on the front of the papers, the murdered woman, she is the woman who came to the house, the one you denied you knew.'

He remained silent.

'I think you owe me an explanation, bring me up to speed, as the boys would say. Were you having an affair with this married woman? Before or whilst we have been together?'

He looked at her and his bloodshot eyes answered her question. 'If the police ask you about her, say nothing. You've never seen her before; she never came to the house.'

'That's not true.'

He fixed her with a hypnotic stare. 'You never saw her.'

She swallowed hard. Trembling, she left the room and went upstairs to get away from him. She wrapped herself in a blanket. She was so cold.

* * *

Hostages in their own home, they remained in separate rooms, silent and unable to comfort each other. He was unreachable. Both were wary of the other, both uncertain of what the other might do or say next. After two days in lockdown, there was a knock at the door, which they ignored until the police car sirens started blaring outside the house. Patrick opened the curtains; the press had been moved a few hundred yards back and they were cordoned off from the road.

He opened the door; two police officers entered. Inspector Jeffers and Sergeant Potts sat down and declined tea or coffee. Surprisingly, they seemed sympathetic to Patrick's situation, hounded by the press and a prisoner in his own home.

'We will manage the press. An officer will be deployed to stop you and your family being accosted. We are here to give an update. We must insist Miss Preston be present.'

Patrick was reluctant to involve her, but he had no choice. Annette, on the other hand, was comforted by the police presence. She knew Patrick would be a fool to harm her whilst a police investigation was in progress. At present, she had nowhere to go to – she had moved away from Manchester, lock, stock, and barrel. She had lost her best friend, Liz, because of Patrick; she had no financial independence, as he hadn't wanted her to work. She was totally reliant on him.

Both officers rose from their seat as Annette entered the room.

'Miss Preston, thank you for joining us to assist us with our enquiries. I am Inspector Jeffers, and this is Sergeant Potts.'

'Hello, ' she said, subdued.

'Are you aware that we are investigating the murder of Mrs Leona Fielding? Mr Clarke told us he had not seen or heard from Mrs Fielding since their relationship ended six months ago.' Inspector Jeffers looked at her closely.

'Miss Preston, you are aware Mr Clarke had a sexual relationship with Mrs Fielding?'

'I… I... Did.' This was new information to her. She tried to compose herself.

'Did you at any time have any contact with Mrs Fielding?'
'No.'

The inspector took a photograph from his file and passed it to her. 'Take a close look.'

Leona was beautiful, sophisticated, and sexy. Annette was jealous of a dead woman. 'No, I have never seen her before.'

Why was she lying? Was it because this woman had pursued her man? Had Patrick murdered her or got someone else to murder her? She stared blankly at the floor.

'We understand this must be putting a lot of stress on both of you, but we will need to speak to both of you again, possibly a number of times. We will visit you if you prefer not to come to the station. Our colleagues in Cheshire are being assisted with their enquiries by the deceased's husband, Mr Fielding, and people close to the couple. Mrs Fielding was estranged from her sister and her parents are both deceased.'

Patrick nodded and remained unusually quiet. Annette wondered if it was guilt or grief.

As the police were about to leave, Justin was being held back by a uniformed officer. Patrick nodded to the officer and said that he was a friend and to allow him through. Justin entered the house, ignored Annette completely, and joined Patrick.

'Patrick, you are on the front of every newspaper. This will relaunch you into the public domain.'

'I can't face rehearsals today, it's all too much to deal with.'

'Jason said to stay home all week if you need to, he understands. Don't stay away too long, or the understudy will be delighted.'

'I don't want a week off. I will go stark raving mad in this house with all its ghosts. I'll be back tomorrow.'

'Stay with me. You would be closer to the theatre and it would be a change of scenery.'

'I would, but it's not a good idea at present, the press has printed all sorts of garbage about me. Resurrected my wife's death, the accident. All I need is that old bastard of a father-in-law to start talking to them, and I don't want Annette to be given any reason to talk to the police.'

'What on earth do you mean? What could she possibly say?'

'She's a bit unstable, possessive, you know what I mean.'

'Indeed, I do. Let's hope she doesn't meet with the same grisly end as Mrs Fielding,' he mumbled under his breath.

'Why haven't you said anything about the murder? You normally love to bitch about Leona,' Patrick said.

'I am a caring, considerate person, that's why. Also, because I couldn't care less what has happened to her. I hated her.'

'Then, someone has done you a very big favour.'

'Not only me, I would think,' Justin added.

* * *

Justin drove to Patrick's, to pick him up at an unearthly four thirty in the morning. They returned to Justin's apartment and stayed there until nine o'clock. Justin served tea and toast.

'Justin, don't fuss so much. I am fine.'

'I have to compete with Lady Annette.'

'There is no need to compete. Annette hasn't so much as asked me how I feel, let alone waited on me hand on foot. Her behaviour is strange at present.'

'Ask her to leave. I can see she no longer makes you happy.'

'It's not that simple.'

'Is it because of the Leona business?'

'Apparently, Leona turned up at the house a while back. I told Annette I didn't know who she was.'

'So, she turned up at the house, so what?'

'I told the police I haven't heard from or seen her for six months.'

'Why?'

'I don't want them to know that she pestered me non-stop. I just wanted her out of my life, but she wouldn't stay away.'

Justin was worried. Why lie to the police?

'Didn't you want her out of my life too?' Patrick asked.

'I did, but I didn't think she would get herself murdered. It's a bit extreme. I didn't murder her.'

'I know you didn't,' Patrick said

Justin began to wonder what if Patrick…

'The last time I saw her, she threatened me.' The fearful tone in Patrick's voice troubled Justin.

'How?'

'By using my son against me.' Patrick paced around the room.

'I don't understand.'

'She screwed one of my sons behind my back. I had to protect my sons.'

'Protect them from what?'

'From her.'

'Do you think not telling the police the truth will protect your sons?'

Patrick didn't answer. Justin was confused.

A silence fell between them.

'Try not to worry about the boys. Matthew has a girlfriend and seems happy. Geoff can look after himself.'

'Will this ever end?' Patrick was forlorn, weary.

'The whole Leona business will eventually blow over. She is no threat to you, me, or your boys. As for Lady Annette, if she tries to spoil our friendship, I will happily break her neck.'

'Would you?' Patrick looked up, alarmed.

'Anything for you.'

* * *

At the theatre, the cast were intrigued to hear what Patrick had to say. Journalists had been tipped off that he would be back at rehearsals, so extra security was provided, and the stage door locked.

'I feel like a fugitive.'

'Nonsense. Think of the publicity for the play.' The director considered that any publicity was good publicity.

'This could finish my career.'

'Everyone will want a ticket for this production.' Gill Richardson had directed Patrick many times over the years; she didn't for one minute consider him capable of murder. Justin also told Patrick he did not believe he was involved in Leona's murder. Patrick found this support encouraging. Although he worried a little why Justin was adamant he knew he was innocent. How could Justin be so certain?'

Annette tried to contact Patrick at the theatre; she was told he did not wish to be disturbed.

* * *

Justin appeared by Patrick's side in the tabloids. He was getting his fifteen minutes of fame and he loved it. He cut out all the photographs of them together. It was wonderful to spend so much time with the man he loved. He relished the publicity. He had become an important person in Patrick's life. He adored the exposure. He was glad Leona was dead. If only Annette would clear off – she was still a thorn in his side.

Justin had to drop Patrick off at his home in Hampstead every evening. Patrick insisted he had to keep an eye on Annette.

Annette and Patrick no longer communicated. He had asked her to sit tight, stay home and speak to no one about Leona. He promised their situation would get better and that she had to trust him. Not a thing he said to her rang true. Since she moved in with Patrick, she had grown from being a trusting woman in search of love to a cynical woman of the world.

Patrick would get by without her – would she get by without him? Dependency on him had led to lack of confidence, whilst being confined to the house had chipped away at who she was, who she once was.

* * *

A small white envelope waited on the doormat, addressed to Annette. She knew what it was. She opened it.

DIE BITCH. DIE.

She felt unable to contact Patrick. Matthew was shacked up with his girlfriend, so instead she rang Geoff, who agreed to drop by. There was no one else she could have called.

He had been at the house only a short time when Inspector Jeffers and Sergeant Potts turned up. Annette was emotionally fraught and close to a breakdown and it was obvious she was falling apart. Geoff led the police officers into the living room.

'The police.'

She was uneasy. Should she tell the police about Leona's visit?

'You look terribly upset, Miss Preston.'

'Show them the letter.' Geoff took the letter from her and passed it to the inspector, who passed it to his sergeant. Both wore a look of concern.

'Did you ever see or speak to Leona Fielding?'

'Yes. She turned up here, only once, months ago. I had no idea who she was.'

'Have you received such a letter before?'

'Yes, there were two other letters, I thought they had stopped.'

Annette started to speak again but stopped herself.

'Tell us all you can,' Potts urged.

'I don't know what else to say. I destroyed the other letters.'

'Why did you not inform the police? Did it not worry you?'

'Yes, I was scared. Patrick didn't take it seriously. He said it was probably a jealous fan and to ignore them.'

'Miss Preston, you were wrong to ignore them. You should have brought them to police attention.'

Geoff was incandescent. 'Dad had no right to put you at risk. A maniac could have sent them.'

Inspector Jeffers looked at them both. 'These letters are significant to our investigation into the murder of Leona Fielding – she, too, was in receipt of such letters. She had kept them in a drawer along with letters she had received from Mr Clarke. Whether or not Mrs Fielding thought the letters were connected, we don't know. It is strange to keep hate mail with letters from an ex-lover.'

'A letter from Dad?'

'Yes. There is no date on the letter and no envelope. It did make reference to a stay at the Priory hospital. Could you tell us when Mr Clarke was admitted and discharged from the Priory? It would help us, with the investigation.'

They both nodded in agreement.

Annette started to shiver. 'Do you think Patrick knew Mrs Fielding was receiving the same letters as me?' she asked.

'How could he if he hadn't heard from or seen her in six months?'

The inspector turned to Geoff. 'Tell me, son, would you know when your father ended the relationship with the deceased?'

Geoff looked at Annette with a sad expression.

'Don't hold back, son, don't try to protect your father.'

'It's not him I'm concerned about. He ended the relationship only days before Annette moved in.'

'What? Those damned knickers.'

'Miss Preston?'

'I found a pair of tarty knickers under the bed. He swore he knew nothing about them.' She turned to Geoff. 'Did she stay over just before I moved in?'

'The odd night. It wasn't my place to say anything.'

'Bastard.' She began to tremble, weeks of tension poured from her eyes.

'You don't need to stay, Miss Preston, we can carry on without you.'

* * *

As soon as Annette left the room, Geoff continued to speak.

'There are things about Dad I don't understand.'

'Go on, son.'

'Lots of strange things have happened. Annette thought the house was haunted. Dad said she might be right. She fell downstairs, whilst Dad was in hospital. Matthew told me the first thing Dad asked was if she was dead. Matthew said that it wasn't the question that bothered him but the way it was said,

131

as if he expected her to be. This would be around the time he wrote to Leona. He was also reluctant to return home.'

'Did Matthew ask him why?'

'Dad told Matthew he too thought the house was haunted. I don't think that was the reason, he simply didn't want to come home.'

'Haunted as in ghosts?'

'Yes.' Geoff laughed nervously.

'What do you think?' asked Jeffers.

'I don't think the house is haunted, but Dad was on a psychiatric ward when he said all this. He was on strong medication, Librium, sleeping tablets.'

'Might that explain his overactive imagination?' said Jeffers.

'He said Annette had experienced the same things.'

'Do you believe her?'

'Yes.'

Jeffers made a few notes.

'My mother's watercolour painting fell off the wall and hit her on the head, then she fell downstairs.'

'Slow down. A painting hit her on the head?'

'Yes. Both she and Dad… both sensed a presence. Nothing tangible.'

'Why do you believe Miss Preston but not your father?'

'Because I don't trust him. Annette said scary things had happened in the house, that ghosts played tricks – it was probably my father or one of his concubines.'

'Do you think your father is capable of hurting Miss Preston? Of putting her life in danger?'

'I have said enough.' Geoff looked uneasy.

'You care about Miss Preston?'

'I guess so. She's not the type my dad usually associates with. She is decent.'

'And Mrs Fielding, was she decent?'

'Not in my opinion.'

'You didn't like her?'

'I didn't know her. I kept out of their way when she stayed over. They were intruders, invaded my mother's memory and decency.'

'Your mother died fifteen years ago. That is a long time to stay faithful to her memory.'

'Dad would never talk about Mum to me and Matthew.'

'It's still painful?'

'Yes,' Geoff said quietly.

Jeffers could see the veil drop over Geoff's eyes; he wouldn't say much more today. So, he changed tactic.

'We interviewed your brother, Matthew, your identical twin. He is very different from you in attitude and mannerisms. He said you were like your father,' Jeffers continued. 'To be precise, he said, "Geoff has many of Dad's traits, most of which are an act. He does it deliberately." Why would he say that?'

'I will have to ask him. I wouldn't try to emulate my father, I am so anti what he is.'

'You do exhibit similar mannerisms.'

'Please, don't liken me to Dad.'

'Your own brother did. He thinks you don't know how to be yourself. That you have yet to find yourself. Have you found yourself?' Jeffers asked with a mocking tone.

Geoff remained silent.

'You strike me as being very protective of your brother, whereas he came across as self-serving.'

'Matthew is a fake. He is really very vulnerable, we both are but would never admit it. We love Dad. We also hate him, probably hate him more than we love him, but he is all we have got. We both blame him for the death of our mother. It was his fault he was drunk, and they were arguing.'

'You were small boys when you lost your mother, four years of age. That is very young to have known the details of the accident.'

Geoff looked up in surprise.

'It is our job as police officers to know the background of the people we interview, to build a picture of their lives.'

'He was blind drunk when he crashed the car, he admitted that. Grandpa has told us everything. Although we were very young, I remember the emptiness and the sense of abandonment. Our mum had gone, and he had been the cause. I might not have had the vocabulary, but I felt the despair and loss and still do.'

'Did any other adult speak with you about your loss?'

'Only Grandpa and Grandma, before Grandma passed away. They were always there for us.'

'Could we have your grandfather's address and telephone number, please?'

'Sure, I'll jot down the details.'

'Thank you, Mr Clarke, you have been a great help in piecing together a picture of the family.'

'Please, call me Geoff. I feel too young to be a Mr Clarke. I hate having the same name as him.'

'Okay, Geoff, we will be in touch if we need to.'

The officers left with more information than they had anticipated. It was a tangled web that Patrick Clarke did weave.

'No wonder Clarke ended up on a psychiatric ward. How does he keep up with all his shenanigans?'

'Beats me, sir.'

CHAPTER TWENTY-THREE

The headlines became racier. *A torrid affair. The love triangle.* The stories portrayed Martin Fielding as the wronged husband. The press got hold of glamour shots Leona had posed for years ago – topless, nude, printed on a double-page spread in all the down-market tabloid newspapers. Leona had never been a successful model, but now she was everywhere, she would have loved it.

One tabloid suggested Patrick Clarke was jinxed. Another headline read, *Murderer or Devil.*

Photographs of Victoria had been resurrected, or rather had been provided by her father. Victoria looked so wholesome and youthful. The story raked over the accident that killed her and a quotation from her father. *Time for the truth.*

Geoff had been approached by the press for comment, an opportunity he had found hard to resist. He gave an account of life with Patrick Clarke and the Clarke-Fielding affair. The tragedy had morphed into a circus and everyone wanted a piece of the action.

Annette tuned into the talk shows, which debated whether or not women who had affairs deserved what they got. *They reap what they sow*, cried the moral majority and religious groups. Because of Annette's fervent jealousy, she felt inclined to agree that they did, whilst she felt a deep pang of guilt.

* * *

Jeffers and Potts arrived at the home of Arthur Vaughan. They already knew the old man hated Clarke and were prepared for some bad-mouthing. They hoped speaking to Vaughan would reveal something about Clarke they were missing. Mr Vaughan welcomed the police officers and immediately began a tirade of accusations.

'Clarke murdered that Fielding woman, not that I have much time for harlots who cheat on their husbands with a piece of shit like Clarke.'

'We are not here to discuss the Fielding case, sir.'

'What are you here for?'

'We want to speak to you about the accident that killed your daughter. If that is all right with you, sir.'

'I am happy to talk about Victoria anytime.'

'We had an interesting conversation with your grandson Geoff. He said he blames his father for the death of his mother.'

'He is right to do so.'

'Would you give us the background history, which led up to the accident?'

'She left him. After years of my wife and I trying to get her to see what a monster he was, she finally saw the light.'

'Why was he a monster?'

'He is an evil, selfish, self-indulgent bastard. Victoria was our only child; she was never any trouble to us. An aspiring young actress, with her whole life ahead of her. Unfortunately, she met Clarke and fell under his spell.'

'Perhaps they simply fell in love?' Potts suggested.

'Love? With Clarke? No, I tell you he is the devil. We tried to reason with her, but she was headstrong, as they are at that age – they know it all. She married him. They married in secret at a registry office, had strangers as witnesses. My wife was heartbroken. Victoria had never been a secretive girl. We brought her up to be honest, but she was under his spell. They moved into the terrace property in Hampstead, where he still lives. Victoria had inherited a bit of money from my father, her grandfather, when he passed away. She used it as the deposit on the house. He squandered whatever money they had. He gambled, mainly card games. He was going out on benders that could last for days, then we found out he cheated on Victoria, with any tart who would give him the eye.'

Jeffers and Potts remained silent.

'We saw a change in her. She lost a lot of weight, became anxious and jumpy. We reached out to her, but she said nothing, kept it all to herself. He broke her heart, yet time and again she forgave him. We were always there to help pick up the pieces. Then, the worst thing that could have happened, did. She was pregnant. I think he got her pregnant on purpose, so she would be dependent on him. He was jealous of her, he didn't want her to succeed in her career, he wanted to be top dog. The pregnancy put an end to her career and things went from bad to worse, but she wouldn't leave him. She was too proud to admit she had made the biggest mistake of her life, marrying him, a whoring bastard.'

'Did things change when she had the boys?'

'Change? His career took off big time. She was left bringing up two babies. We helped, but it was hard for us to help raise his babies, but we did. It took another three years for the scales to fall from her eyes. She left him, brought the boys and moved in with us. An ideal arrangement. It is a big house and we loved them being with us, safe and free of him. Victoria saw a solicitor and was filing for divorce. Clarke pleaded with her not to divorce him, he begged her to return home. He eventually accepted she was serious and wanted him out of her life. He told her he would sign the papers if she would meet him to discuss access to the boys. When she agreed to do so, she sealed her fate. I tried my hardest to persuade her not to meet him. Clarke had convinced her he was true to his word. She went to meet him, and we never saw her alive again. Our biggest fear was that she would take him back, we never imagined the outcome would be her death. He murdered our daughter. He had no intention of signing those divorce papers. He killed her, the drunken, evil bastard. He took her life.'

Tears welled in the elderly man's eyes.

'The verdict should have been at least manslaughter, but he walked free. A suspended sentence for two years, because he was over the limit when the accident occurred. His legal team used the sympathy card – he had lost his wife, he would never forgive himself, he was responsible for two little boys who needed their father. It helped his case that he was an aspiring actor. People fall for all that rubbish.'

'I am very sorry,' said Jeffers.

'Five years later, my wife died. She was never the same after we lost Victoria. It killed a part of us both. I shall keep going until I see Clarke pay. I intend to haunt him for the rest of his days. He will have no peace whilst I'm alive.'

'Your hate of Clarke must have impacted on your grandsons?'

'No doubt they feel as guilty as hell for maintaining contact with him. But, you see, he has no house rules, he allows them free rein, to run loose, there has never been any house rules to abide by in that house of sin.'

'Maybe they love their father?' Potts bravely added.

'Love him? Love him be damned. They have nothing but contempt for him.'

CHAPTER TWENTY-FOUR

Justin scooped up his mail and a small white envelope caught his eye. He opened it.

PREPARE TO DIE.

Upset and shaken, he screwed up the piece of paper and threw it against the wall. Then he left for the theatre.

* * *

Patrick and Annette made a pact that they would face the press side by side, front it out. Patrick was now able to travel to the theatre without getting mobbed; he had cooperated with the press as much as he was allowed to – he was still a suspect in a murder inquiry. He decided it was time to distance himself from Justin, at least until all this was over. What he needed was positive press. He needed to cultivate a relationship with the pack that sat outside his door. Patrick was happy to use Justin as a scapegoat to win Annette over.

'I promise Justin will never again step over the threshold. I will sacrifice my friendship with Justin to prove my love and commitment to you. In return, I must insist you promise not to tell the police of any of your suspicions, regarding anyone.'

Annette represented normality, wholesomeness. After all, how could a young, intelligent woman like Annette Preston live with a murderer? Perfect. But Patrick worried Justin might speak to the press about their intimate relationship. He must never be allowed to do that.

* * *

Justin had been exiled. He found it hard to accept. Annette had seen him watching the house; their eyes would lock, and he would stare her out. She was convinced he was going to kill her. Of course, Patrick told her not to overreact, but this time she refused to stay in the solitary confinement of four walls. There was only one way Patrick would sit up and take notice. So she packed her bag, put AP on a lead, and left.

* * *

Patrick arrived home very late. He thought it was strangely quiet, and the house was in darkness. He assumed Annette had gone to bed and taken AP with her. He stoked up the fire, poured himself a whisky and lit a cigarette. He lay back on the sofa, closed his eyes and relaxed in the silence and stillness of the night.

He woke at three in the morning and went upstairs to bed, to find Annette had gone. He panicked. He raced from room to room, put on all the lights in the house, even looked under the stairs. He feared she had been murdered and bunged into some dark corner. The image of Annette battered and bleeding stuck in his mind. He rushed back upstairs, coughing, short of breath, and checked the wardrobes. Nothing. He reached for a small, black leatherbound box and took a solitary key from it. He threw the box on the bed and raced to the room at the end of the landing, the room that scared him. He opened the door and groped around for the light switch and tripped on the bare floorboards. Something jabbed into his arm. He scrambled to his feet and lurched towards the wall – finally, he switched the light on, and let out a sigh of relief. The light bulb gave out a dim glow. It lit up the centre of the room but not the edges. Victoria's memorabilia boxed up and piled high, all her books, photo albums, hairbrushes, clothes, and shoes, all covered in cobwebs. The smell of dampness and neglect got to the back of his throat. He was ashamed of himself for locking all her belongings away. He had kept them from the boys, denied she had ever existed. Through fear he had locked away any sign of her and tried to stamp her out of their memories.

Patrick thought he was headed for another breakdown; he should never have gone back on the booze. He had imagined Annette had been murdered by Victoria and her body dumped in this room, the room to which only he had a key. Victoria was never evil or vengeful. She would never have contemplated murder in this life or the afterlife, and she would never haunt the house her sons called home. He was still terrified he might see her spirit. There was blood on his arm – a few splinters had dug into his flesh. He left the room and locked the door.

* * *

He checked Annette's wardrobe and noted some of her clothes had been taken. He came to the conclusion she had left of her own accord. He remembered what she had said about Justin watching the house, and he recalled Justin had said he would happily kill her. What if Justin had forced his way into the house and coerced her into leaving him? Patrick picked up his jacket, got in his car and sped off to Justin's flat. At four o'clock in the morning, the roads were empty. He rang the intercom and banged on the outside door until a resident let him in. He took the stairs two at a time. He was outside the

143

flat and he banged on the door like a man possessed. No reply. Justin must be away. On his way back to the car, he considered giving Annette's mother a call, but changed his mind, not wanting a lecture on how he had corrupted her daughter and what a disappointment he was.

When Annette hadn't returned the next day, he informed the police. Patrick feared the worst.

* * *

Geoff had moved back home with his father for the time being. He was elated to be allowed to go into the room with all his mother's possessions. He spent hours going through old photographs of the family they once were. For the first time he felt he was home and that his family was truly coming back together.

Geoff, full of enthusiasm, took the albums downstairs and joined his father in front of the fire.

'Look, Dad, I've got two albums full of photos of you and Mum, me and Matthew when we were babies. Look at this one of you and Mum before you got married – you were so skinny.'

* * *

They talked for hours, the photographs spread across the floor. Patrick shared the past with a son who hungered for his family history. Patrick saw the glow in his son's eyes; he was like a child at Christmas, when the atmosphere is full of magic, hope and anticipation. He recalled the little boy he had abandoned emotionally, who he had failed to care for and protect. He could almost reach out and touch him. With an agonising lurch in his stomach, the moment passed as quickly as the years had. Geoff was still talking enthusiastically; Patrick only just managed to swallow back a cry of sorrow as their eyes met.

The telephone rang.

'Dad, leave it,' Geoff pleaded, not wanting to break the magic, not wanting the outside world of reality to invade the peaceful atmosphere of their rediscovered past.

'I have to, it could be information about Annette.'

He frowned. Why was his father bothered about her when they were sharing warm memories of his mother? The anger started to swirl.

'Geoff, the police have found Annette.' Patrick was visibly relieved.

'Oh,' Geoff mumbled. He looked down.

'I thought you would be pleased.'

'I am.'

'Aren't you going to ask where she is?'

Geoff's irritation started to rise. 'Where is she?'

'She is with her friend, Liz.'

Geoff tried to push down his irritation and recapture the intimacy they had had before the phone call.

'Hey, Dad, look at this.' He held up a photograph of Matthew and himself shortly after they had been born.

Patrick took the photograph from him.

'My goodness, I remember this being taken. I was terrified of holding you both, you were so small and fragile.'

* * *

There was a photograph of them all together, 'Victoria and her boys' written on the back of it. He could hold back the tears no longer. A cry of grief expelled from his throat. Patrick fell to his knees. Geoff rushed forwards and cradled his father in his arms.

'You really cared,' Geoff spluttered through his own tears.

He so wished he could start again. Another woman, another family. He wouldn't make the same mistakes second time around.

CHAPTER TWENTY-FIVE

The police had been alerted to 14 Carlton Court, an address in a block of private apartments. Neighbours had been complaining of a foul smell coming from the flat on the second floor.

Two officers broke down the door. Within seconds they were gagging from the stench. Forensics took over and began to gather evidence. Inspector Jeffers and Sergeant Potts, masked and gowned, joined the forensic team as they proceeded to investigate.

* * *

Patrick called Liz and begged her to let him speak to Annette. She did eventually take his call, secretly pleased he had persisted. She missed him so much. It had been awful, skulking back to Liz and Gerry, after everything that had happened, and with a dog in tow. They had let her stay with them as she had nowhere else to go. She had bitten her tongue and let them say such terrible things about Patrick; she had to sit back and let it wash over her.

Patrick was right about one thing: Gerry was not the man she had thought he was. He had always appeared mild-mannered and easy-going, but he had an unhealthy obsession with Patrick's personal life, which she found disconcerting.

'Annette, I have been out of my mind with worry. Please come home.'

'I want to be with you, but I don't want to spend so much time alone in that house.'

'I promise you won't be alone in the house. I will take time off work, give the understudy a break, and Geoff has moved back in.'

'Geoff's with you?'

Annette desperately wanted to leave Liz and Gerry's and she didn't wish to return north to live with her mother. This was music to her ears.

Annette agreed to go home. The news did not go down well with Liz and Gerry. She appeased them on the pretence she needed her clothes and personal belongings.

* * *

Annette woke up next to the man she loved. She was pleased to be away from Gerry and his negative rants. She decided not to tell Patrick about the things Gerry had said.

The two of them took AP for a walk on the heath and let him off the lead. He enjoyed a run, bounding across the open space, and loved to meet other canine friends. It was cold and crisp; spring was on its way. A time for fresh starts.

'You were right about Gerry. He and Liz are not as loved-up as I thought. She is scared to speak up or contradict him. She is in denial about something. Do you know what I mean?'

'Yes.'

'He is very preoccupied with you.'

'Me?' Patrick looked uncomfortable. 'I wonder why?'

'I thought you might be able to tell me.'

'Some things are best left alone.'

'What do you mean by that?'

'There are certain things you don't need to know. It would change things if you did.'

'A big dark secret?'

'Let sleeping dogs lie.' He put his hands in his pockets and took a deep breath. He strolled ahead to look for AP. Annette stood in silence; her insides somersaulted. She considered a couple of reasons for Gerry's preoccupation and concluded each one was as unbearable as the other. She decided not to pursue this any further, in case her hunch was true. She caught up with Patrick, put her arm through his.

'There is just one more thing I want to say.'

'Spit it out, woman.'

'I still don't want that Justin chap to come to the house again. I don't feel safe near him.'

'Don't worry about Justin. I haven't set eyes on him in weeks. He won't bother either of us again.'

He kissed her, and then they strolled down to the lake as AP bounded on ahead.

They agreed to be honest with each other. Their relationship was full of love and affection, and they were closer than they had ever been. Even with the Leona Fielding murder investigation still ongoing, Patrick tried to be jovial and attentive.

Back at the house, Patrick wanted a word with his son.

'Geoff,' he called, before turning to Annette. 'Put the kettle on, sweetheart.'

Patrick went upstairs. He knocked on the bedroom door and entered.

'He's gone – back to his student accommodation, I assume. Which means we have the house to ourselves.'

'Wonderful. Peace and tranquillity.'

The telephone rang and Annette took the call.

'Inspector Jeffers speaking. Is Mr Clarke at home?'

'Yes, do you want to speak to him?'

'No, we will come to speak with him face to face. Should be with you in fifteen minutes.'

'I'll let him know.'

The familiar queasiness in the pit of her stomach returned; her joy drained away. She told Patrick the police were on their way.

'That's all we need.'

* * *

The police officers arrived, and they all sat down.

'Have you caught the killer?'

'No. I am afraid we have bad news for you, sir.' Patrick's heart thudded.

'It's not one of the boys?'

'Calm yourself, sir. This isn't about your sons. It is regarding your friend Justin Sharp.'

'Why are you bothering me about Justin?'

'We were led to believe you were close.'

'We are colleagues, fellow actors, we aren't close friends. I haven't seen him in weeks. He never turned up at the theatre; no one could get hold of him. We thought he had gone AWOL. Cleared off.'

'I am sorry to tell you Justin Sharp went nowhere. He is dead.'

Patrick and Annette looked at each other in disbelief. Patrick's mouth fell open. He managed, 'How?'

'He has been murdered. He met with a very brutal end.'

'Murdered? Who would want to murder Justin?'

'That is what we intend to find out.' Jeffers looked directly at Patrick. 'Can you think of anyone who might be able to assist us?'

'Have a word with the cast?'

'What about his friends?'

'I never met any of Justin's social circle.'

Patrick did not want the press to find out about his relationship with Justin. If his relationship with Justin got out to the press with all the publicity and the fearmongering around the AIDS outbreak, his career would be doomed. As for Annette, she would never understand. She had led a sheltered life – she took the *Daily Mail*, for goodness' sake.

'Mr Sharp was homosexual.'

'What of it?' Patrick's eyes fixed on Jeffers.

'You were close to him. Do you know if he was in a relationship? Or who his homosexual friends were?'

'I have just said I have no idea.'

'Was he inclined to engage in casual sexual liaisons, one-night stands?'

'How the hell should I know?'

'What about family?'

'I have no idea about his family or his lifestyle.'

'Were you not intrigued to know a little more about your friend's life?'

'No. I had no interest in his private life, only his artistic talent.' Even to himself, his response did not ring true.

The officers looked unconvinced.

'We shall need to interview you at some point, Mr Clarke, formally. It will involve questions of a more personal nature. Whoever murdered Mrs Fielding is no doubt the same person who murdered Mr Sharp. The killer used the same method of mutilation, his or her calling card, so to speak. Both of the victims are connected to you, one way or another. Before we leave this for now, there is something else that links the victims and Miss Preston.'

She gulped. 'Me?'

'We searched Mr Sharp's apartment. We found a couple of letters. They contained the same written death threats received by Mrs Fielding and yourself, Miss Preston.'

The nightmare continued. Patrick paused thoughtfully, and then said, 'There is someone who didn't care for Justin. His name is Gerry Scott, stage manager at the Hammersmith Armchair Theatre. Annette said, only recently, there was something about him that was amiss.'

She shot Patrick a look.

'I don't for one minute think Gerry is capable of murder.'

The officers listened intently.

'You know this man, Gerry Scott?'

'I am a friend of his wife. I only know Gerry through Liz. Gerry wouldn't kill anyone. I don't think you should involve them.'

'Let the police decide who needs to be questioned,' Patrick retorted.

She suddenly blurted out, 'Perhaps Mr Clarke wishes to offload his own guilt.'

A silence fell. She began to squirm. 'I didn't mean what I just said. I'm upset by all this death and uncertainty.'

Patrick could not bring himself to look at her. Annette had betrayed him.

* * *

The police left.

Previously Patrick had asked Geoff, in a roundabout way, about Leona, the times she had stayed over. From what Geoff said it was unlikely he had had sex with Leona. He despised her. Which meant it must have been Matthew. Patrick had ignored Matthew since he realised he had had sex with Leona. Petty jealousy had caused him to push his son out of his life.

Patrick flew into action. He drove to Matthew's place. He needed to know if Matthew had anything to do with the murders. If he had, it was his own fault for failing his boy.

He pulled up outside the house. The door was open. As he entered, he was greeted by smoke and numerous young people drinking cheap wine. Matthew was sprawled across the sofa with his arm around his girlfriend's shoulder.

'Dad, what are you doing here?' They went into the kitchen. Patrick gave Matthew an update on the murder inquiry.

'Justin's murder is believed to have been carried out by the same person who murdered Leona.'

Patrick studied his son's face for traces of guilt.

'Gosh, Dad, that's terrible. I have followed Leona's case in the newspapers. You looked good on the front pages.' He laughed.

'Matthew, this is serious. Two people have been murdered, both linked to me.'

'What does it have to do with me?' He looked bewildered. 'Did you drive here especially to tell me about Justin? It will be in all the papers tomorrow. I could have read about it. Why do I need to be told face to face? Why would I be interested in

153

what has happened to either of them other than from a news point of view? I didn't know them the way you did, none of this has anything to do with me. As for Leona, I barely saw her.'

'Are you sure about that?'

'Absolutely.'

'Sorry to have disturbed your afternoon. I can see you are busy with friends and new girlfriend.'

'She's great. We started off as friends and it's kind of developed.'

'I'll let you get back to them. It was good to see you.'

'And you, Dad.'

Patrick drove home unconvinced. Matthew had had sex with Leona and had said nothing. Leona could have made it up? Matthew was cool and collected. It niggled him – how well did he know his son? Patrick had become a little closer to Geoff recently. They had turned a corner in their relationship and become much friendlier, but Matthew was different. He was not as emotional as Geoff.

Matthew was extroverted, outgoing – he had become a bit cocky. Had Matthew hoodwinked him? He would do anything to protect his son. Matthew's life had just begun. He was young, handsome – he would one day be a fine, successful man. No one and nothing was going to stop his son living his life to the full.

* * *

Patrick didn't want to go home, but there was nowhere else to go. He despised Annette for what she had said to the police. Did she really think he was covering his tracks, that he might be the perpetrator? He might cover up for Matthew, but she had implicated him in a cover-up of his own misdoings.

He entered the house. AP ran towards him, full of energy and joy, unaware of the decimation of his family and relationship. He saw his reflection in the mirror. *God, I look old. I look like a vagrant, unwashed and unshaven.* He retreated to his study with a bottle, put on the classical radio station, and closed the door on the world.

* * *

Annette made sure to keep out of his way. She could not face him after what she had told the police. They had rekindled their relationship and she had blown it all away.

She couldn't see a way back this time.

It seemed to spell the end.

* * *

The next day, they were bombarded with telephone calls and the press resumed their invasion of the area. Justin's murder was another nail in the coffin for Patrick.

Gerry Scott was incandescent with rage. Patrick had implicated Gerry in the murders of Leona and Justin. Gerry had been taken to the police station and questioned for hours; he had had to account for his whereabouts, on the dates and estimated times of both murders. The police had taken his diary. All his evidence had yet to be corroborated.

'I told you, Annette, he was no good, but to involve me in a murder investigation is a step too far. We took you in, when you had nowhere to go, and what thanks to we get? I have never heard of this Leona Fielding. On no account darken our doorstep again. Your friendship with Liz is over. All you have brought us is trouble and heartache.'

Annette was sick to her stomach, her life disintegrated before her eyes. Then a second telephone call, this one from her mother.

'It's time for you to come home. Why are you staying with a man who might have murdered two people? You could be next.'

'I can't just leave in the middle of an ongoing investigation. I'm involved whether I like it or not. I will keep you updated when I know something. Don't worry, Mum, I'm safe.'

Annette knew, the way things were headed, she would have to move in with her mother; it might be the only option available to her. She was dizzy with anxiety. Her doctor had prescribed a mild tranquiliser; she took one and lay on the bed. She relaxed and switched off from the chaos.

CHAPTER TWENTY-SIX

Patrick had been brought in for questioning. He thought he might be arrested for the murders at any time. He had been at the station for hours. The manner in which they questioned him caused him concern. The police believed he was connected to both murders and he feared they might be right. Fortunately, they had not implicated Matthew.

Jeffers, and Potts, left him alone in the interview room. For twenty minutes he sat and stared at the wall, his mind deadened. The door burst open.

'You are free to leave, Mr Clarke.' Jeffers was preoccupied. 'We will be in touch.'

Patrick fixed Jeffers with a resentful stare. 'Just like that?'

'As I said, we will be in touch.'

He sensed they had a new lead, new information.

Patrick bolted from the police station. He drove wildly until he arrived at his destination.

He switched off the engine and ran towards the house. Uniformed police had already surrounded the premises. His father-in-law came out of the house with a shotgun.

'I should have used this on you years ago,' he spat.

A silence fell between the two men. Geoff came out of the house to join his grandfather. The three of them stood in silence. The police held back.

Patrick was confused.

'Where is Matthew?' Patrick shouted.

The old man remained silent. Geoff smiled at his father.

'Tell Matthew to come out of the house,' he called out again.

Patrick wanted to ensure his son wasn't shot for resisting arrest. He began to yell.

'Matthew, get out here. We have got to sort this out.'

He jumped, shocked as a large black van sped up to the house and skidded to a halt. The armed response unit did not intend to take any further risks. Armed police, in black bulletproof vests and helmets, charged from the vehicle and surrounded the house.

Patrick was startled at the level of backup that accompanied the uniformed officers.

Jeffers and Potts approached Patrick.

'What's going on?' he asked.

Jeffers gave him a sympathetic smile and replied quietly, 'It's over.'

Jeffers proceeded to the front gate; he walked along the path until he reached Geoff.

'Come along, son. The game's up.'

Patrick saw what was playing out, in slow motion.

'You have got it wrong, Inspector. This isn't Matthew, it's Geoff.'

'I know who it is, sir. Come along, young man.'

Geoff smiled. He refused to move. His grandfather raised the shotgun.

'Please, put the gun down, sir. You are surrounded by armed police officers.'

Patrick would not be silenced. 'Inspector Jeffers, this is Geoff. It's not Matthew. You have the wrong son.'

'Please, Mr Clarke, kindly step back and let us do our job.'

Geoff stepped forwards, looked at his father, and calmly said, 'I did it.'

'No, no, you don't know what you are saying.' Patrick was beside himself with confusion and disbelief.

'Don't cover up for your brother. Don't take the blame for what he has done.'

Patrick turned to his father-in-law. 'Do something, you stupid old man. Tell them Geoff didn't do it.'

His father-in-law shook his head and threw the shotgun to the ground.

'You are as guilty as my son.' Patrick screamed at the elderly man.

'Don't blame Grandpa. I did it, I killed them both.' Geoff continued to smile at his father. 'Go on, Dad. Ask me why?'

Patrick was a complete wreck as the truth filtered through his senses. 'Why did you kill them?'

'They were vile creatures, who defiled our mother's memory. I gave them three opportunities to leave us alone.'

'The letters?' Patrick said.

'Yes. I sent the letters, they didn't work. Those people still returned to our home. What else was I supposed to do?'

'Annette received the letters too.'

Geoff smiled and shrugged.

'The paranormal activity in the house?'

'Me.'

'Annette falling down the stairs?'

'A hat-trick. Me every time.'

Patrick shuddered.

His father-in-law, grief-stricken, looked at his grandson and placed his hand on the boy's shoulder.

'I did it for us, Grandpa.'

'I know you did what you thought was right. It is time you went along with the police and tell them everything. Will you do that, Geoff?'

'Yes, Grandpa. Will you come with me?'

'No. They want to talk to you. I will join you later.'

The enormity of what had happened silenced everyone.

Geoff walked towards the police and was escorted away.

'This is down to you, Clarke.' The old man spat. 'A debase, decadent devil. You killed my daughter, destroyed your son – this is all your doing.'

Furious, Patrick could endure no more. 'Not all my doing. You have had a hand in this tragedy. Fed the lad all your hatred. Remember what Geoff has said. He did it for you. Do you think Victoria will be able to rest more peacefully now?'

Patrick walked back to his car, weighed down with the despair and emptiness he had felt when Victoria died. Now he carried the additional burden for Geoff and for the victims. The victims whose only failing was to care for him. Perhaps the old man was right, maybe he was a devil.

But would a devil feel the remorse and guilt that engulfed him? He was no devil, he was a man, a human being, with shortcomings and inadequacies, all part of the human condition.

Patrick made a promise to Victoria and to himself. This time he would not run away or hide from the pain, but face it all head-on, without the booze or the vices. If the burden destroyed him, so be it. He would not shirk from his responsibilities, as a father and a man.

It was time to face up to his responsibilities.

It was time to face his demons.

You cannot change your past, but you can learn from it. And eventually live with it.

The End

THE AUTHOR

Julie Conrad lives in Cheshire with her husband and three Pomeranian dogs. With a long career as a social worker in London boroughs before returning to the north west to practice. In 1997 she became a Regulatory Inspector for an Inspection unit now CQC.

BA[Hons]Social Science degree plus CQSW. Middlesex University.

BA[Hons}Regulation and Inspection. University of Salford.

An acrylic artist, member of the Altrincham Society of Artists for ten years. Julie has had two private exhibitions as well as exhibiting with the ASA.

Loves all animals and wildlife, gardening, growing vegetables and very tall tulips.

An avid fitness fan for over forty years. Julie remains a vibrant, creative person who promotes and supports animal welfare, RSPCA, PETA, and kindness to all.

Lightning Source UK Ltd.
Milton Keynes UK
UKHW040757201121
394268UK00004B/1189